Eye Candy

Sonia Hayes

N.U.A

N.U.A

**NATIONAL
UNDERGROUND
ASSOCIATION**

NUA Multimedia
2657-G Annapolis Road
Suite 233
Hanover, MD 21076

Cover Art by Craig "The Flux" Singleton
Cover design by Diane Florence
Author Portrait by Ron MacDonald

ISBN: 978-0-9777573-2-9

Library of Congress Control Number: 2008921255

This book is dedicated to:

The young ladies of the Boys and Girls Club of Greater Milwaukee, your stage play production of "Ms. Thang" was awesome and I thank you from the bottom of my heart. Thank you to all the Delta Academy young ladies and Delta Gems, and all the participants from the YWCA, Boys and Girls Clubs of America, and Girl Scouts of America programs throughout the country. You make my journey worthwhile. To the wonderful mentors whom I have met on my life's journey, thank you for taking the time to pour back into our most precious commodity, our youth. Thank you for all the ways you encourage and inspire our young people. Thank you to the numerous teachers and high school administrators across the country for finding enough value in my novels to share with your precious gems, your students.

Acknowledgments

Super Trooper, thank you for all your encouragement along the rocky road to publishing. You truly have been my biggest supporter, but more importantly, I thank you for being my life partner. To one of the most intelligent young ladies I know, Sonia P., what mother could ask for more! My darlings, Sasha and Savanna, you fuel me and drain me (smile), but you two are so worth it. But do you think you could go at least a day without fighting? And to auntie's "Tekipoo" (Tiekela), my sweet Kirah, and handsome Khari, I love you all dearly. Sybal Jackson, Milwaukee's finest, thank you for assisting me on my book tours across the country. Trish Mitchell, thank you for being the only friend willing to drive around with my magnet on your car. If that ain't love! Lucy B.A.W.W., I know you love me because you put up with me and my mess. Remember Thanksgiving 2007, ha, ha ha! AEP3, thank you so much for taking the time to read and edit my works and for keeping the babies while we vacationed, you are the best father-in-law a girl could ask for. To my editor, Ann Fisher, thank you for the great edits, but mostly I thank you for your enthusiasm and encouragement. Last but not least, thanks to all my tried and true fans for your constant inquiries regarding *Eye Candy*. This is for you. **Enjoy!**

Eye Candy

Chapter 1

Scorching sun rays beamed down on Brittany, Natasha and Shaniqua as the three best friends ate lunch in the lush green courtyard of Miller Grove High School. The excitement of spring break sparkled in everyone's eyes. In a couple of days, students would be out of school for the one-week vacation. Brittany flipped her long, wavy locks to one side. "So, Tasha, are you all packed?"

Natasha nodded through a forkful of salad while perspiration beaded on her forehead. "Girl, please, are you?"

"I'm not taking any clothes, only a couple of empty oversized suitcases. I plan on doing a lot of shopping," Brittany said, letting her deep dimples frame her perfect smile.

Shaniqua toyed with her red Razr phone. "Oh yeah, Tasha, I get paid Friday, so I'm going to give you some money to bring me back a cute outfit from Paris."

"Ohmigod, hide!" Natasha said, ducking behind Shaniqua. "Here comes Stephen—pretend like you don't see him."

Brittany frowned. "Girl, why are you trying to dodge your man?"

"Because he wants to be up under me all the time."

Shaniqua stood up and yelled across the courtyard. "Stephen! Tasha wants you."

"Dang!" Natasha scolded. "Why'd you do that?"

"Because I get tired of you frontin' like you're not really into him."

"If I am, it's my business and if I'm not, it's my business!" Natasha said, then flashed a fake smile at Stephen who was coming quickly toward her. "Hey, what's up?"

"What's up, ladies?" Stephen said. He kissed his girlfriend on the cheek. "I've been looking all over for you."

Natasha let out a soft, sarcastic chuckle. "Well, you found me."

Suddenly, a group of senior class boys walked past the table. Adonis, the tallest of the group, called out, "What's up, Tasha?"

Excitement fueled her smile until she realized her boyfriend was sitting right next to her. Stephen looked slowly from Natasha to Adonis and then back to Natasha. "Who's that?"

She shook her head, hoping to shake out a response but nothing came. "Who him?" she said, trying to hide the fact that she was blushing.

Brittany snickered, creating even more tension.

"Him who, Tasha?" Stephen said. His tone was as hard as the concrete bench he was sitting on.

"Adonis is in PE with me."

"Why did he go all out to speak to you, but didn't speak to anyone else at the table?"

Brittany looked back and forth between Natasha and Stephen, then stood up and started singing Nelly's song, "It's getting hot in here!"

No one acknowledged the joke. It was obvious that the tension was very real between them. Brittany offered an apologetic smile. "All right, Tasha, I'll holla! Shaniqua, are you coming?"

Shaniqua looked at Brittany as if she had completely lost her mind. "I'm not done eating, yet," she said, then casually crossed her legs and slid the tip of a French fry in her mouth. Her expression showed that this was better drama than anything staged on the Jerry Springer Show.

"Shaniqua, let's go!"

She rolled her eyes hard at Brittany and slowly grabbed her belongings, then waved goodbye to Natasha.

As soon as Natasha's friends were far enough away, Stephen rose from the bench, crossed his arms over his chest and just stared down at his girlfriend. His hazel eyes seemed to darken with anger like two mood rings. "What's up, Tasha? You have something you want to tell me?"

"What are you talking about?"

"What's up with you and Aladdin?"

"Adonis! And nothing's up with us. We're just friends."

"Yeah, alright."

"Yeah, alright," Natasha snapped back. She grabbed her belongings. "I've got to get to PE."

"To see Aladdin?"

Natasha flicked him off with her hand. He wasn't even worth correcting. She couldn't admit this to her friends, but Stephen was really beginning to irritate her with his paranoid ways. The week before, he had scrolled through her cell phone when she left her purse on the seat next to him in the movie theater. When she unexpectedly returned to her seat, he reasoned that he was just trying to see the time.

The locker room was filled with girls changing into shorts and tee shirts for class. No matter how often the janitors cleaned the room, it still bore the smell of a damp, musty basement that had been closed up for years. Natasha quickly changed and made her way into the gymnasium where she noticed a little man, who had to be at least ninety years old, had replaced Coach Gilmore. He blew a whistle to exert his authority, pulled up his polyester light blue pants around his protruding belly. "My name's

Coach Luebke. Coach Gilmore isn't here today."

Someone yelled out, "No, duhhh!" Everyone laughed and cracked more jokes.

Coach Luebke ignored them and continued, "I'm declaring today a free play. Whatever equipment you use, be sure to sign for it."

Students immediately scattered across the gym. Most girls took to the bleachers to get their fill of gossip for the day. Natasha had no interest. Gossiping with the wrong crew was messy. She had her trusted sources for gossip, so she signed out a basketball and found a little hoop off to the side so that she would not interfere with the game the boys were running. She jumped for a lay-up when all of a sudden the ball went sailing through the air like a kite across the gym. "Get that out of here!" She heard someone shout. When her feet touched back down on the floor, she quickly noticed who was behind the shot block. "Adonis, quit playing!"

"What, I can't play with you?" Adonis wore his smile like a badge of honor. Most other boys smiled like it hurt or like they had given up smiling altogether.

"Nope!"

Adonis grabbed his chest. "Ahh, man, you breaking my heart."

Natasha bit her lip to conceal her smile. "Boohoo, cry me a river!"

"That's cold, girl, that's cold."

"Yo, Adonis, let's run it, man!" somebody called out.

"Eh, girl, I'm watchin' you!" Adonis said with his shapely lips curled into a smile and his index finger directed at his eye. His athletic physique sprinted down the court. The gold practice jersey contrasted nicely against his smooth, dark skin.

Natasha found herself smiling. He was a serious catch. Taller than her height of 5' 10". Not too many boys in the school towered over her. Definitely a plus, she thought. She had seen Adonis over the years, but never gave him much thought because he always had a girlfriend. She looked around the gymnasium discreetly, hoping no one had witnessed the exchange. Practically everyone in the school knew that she went out with Stephen. If word got back to Stephen that she and Adonis were playing ball together, there would definitely be drama that she definitely didn't need at the end of her high school years. She grabbed her ball and continued shooting around, resisting the temptation to gaze at Adonis.

Chapter 2

Shaniqua made her way to class; envy coursing through her because her best friends were going to France without her. Now that she had a job, cell phone, cute clothes on her back, and money in her pocket, her friends were still ahead of her. She couldn't figure out if Brittany was purposely annoying her or if she was just being "Bragadocious Brittany." For weeks, Brittany had seized every opportunity to talk about how she and Natasha were going to be "kickin' it" in another country without their parents around and how this trip was going to be something they would remember for the rest of their lives. To hear it, was like someone pouring salt on an open wound, burning Shaniqua's flesh, dissolving her to bare bones. Her friends were traveling out of the country while she had never ventured outside of Georgia. Granny never even took them to the family reunions in Alabama because of transportation limitations. She would say, "People always robbin' folks on the bus, and if God had intended for us to fly, he woulda gave us wings."

Shaniqua plopped down in a seat, thinking if only she

had joined the International Studies group along with her friends during freshman year. But it had seemed like a total waste of time. Only nerds did stuff like that. She had chosen Spanish to satisfy the minimum language requirements for graduation. If only she had chosen French and stuck with it for four years, she'd be going to France with Brittany and Natasha. Money wasn't even that big of a deal. Brittany's parents were paying her way, but Natasha and many other students had sought sponsorships to help offset the cost of the trip.

When the school day ended, Shaniqua made her way to the job that she had held since junior year. One good thing about spring break was that her manager had already agreed to let her work full-time at the clothing store. A privilege that Teen Express extended to all seniors who worked there so they could earn extra money for college. Maybe she would try to buy herself a car with the extra cash. Brittany had a new Honda Accord that she had gotten last year at her sweet sixteen party. Natasha drove her dad's old car, but Shaniqua frequented the bus.

Hot fashions along with loud hip-hop music drove girls into the popular store. It was already filled with students looking for outfits for spring break when

Shaniqua offered the assistant manager, Ursula, a phony smile and then went into the back room. Ursula trailed her back there. "Uh, what time were you supposed to be here?" Ursula asked with annoyance.

Shaniqua kept her back to Ursula. She didn't feel like getting into verbal combat with a semi-fashionable wildebeest today. Every time they worked together there was some type of drama—either Shaniqua didn't do something right or she wasn't being polite to the customers. She drew in a deep breath. "Four o'clock. Why?"

"Because you're late. Don't let it happen again."

Shaniqua looked down at her watch. It was just a couple of minutes after four. She turned around and stared at Ursula, slapping her with her eyeballs. Ursula was a short, plump woman. Shaniqua hated to call the woman ugly. Granny would say, "It ain't right to talk about folks. God don't like ugly. Folks can't help the way theys born." But Ursula could help it. She didn't have to have bleached blond hair. It just didn't look good with darker complexions. Shaniqua's eyes traveled down the assistant manager's cellulite-dented thighs, down her thick ankles and then to Ursula's plump toes where big crusty bunions were bursting out of her strappy stilettos. *Tore up from the floor up!* Shaniqua rolled her eyes heavenward because it was going to take the grace of God to keep from saying something. She shoved her purse in the locker and went back out on the floor.

"Excuse me," a voice called from the fitting room.

Shaniqua draped a pair of jeans across her shoulder and walked over. "Yes?"

The girl smiled and then handed Shaniqua the pants that didn't fit. "I need a size five, please."

Shaniqua grabbed the pants while the girl was standing there in her underwear with the door wide open. She wondered how shoppers could so easily reveal themselves to complete strangers while she quickly exchanged the pants and handed them to the customer.

"Could you please stand here for just a moment to tell me how they look?" the girl pleaded.

"Sure." Shaniqua busied herself by straightening out some shirts on a nearby rack.

The fitting room door swung open. "Well, how do they look?" the girl asked, turning around to give Shaniqua a good view of her shapely, petite frame.

Shaniqua offered the same indifferent nod as she did most times when she didn't feel like engaging the customer. "Cute."

"Oh, really." The girl's wide smile displayed the piercing underneath her lip. It wiggled. "So you like the jeans or you like the way they fit on me?"

Shaniqua scrunched her face in confusion. She didn't want to be rude. "They're cute and they look nice on you."

"Thank you. What's your name?"

"Shaniqua."

"You're cute." The girl extended her dainty hand. "My name's Fabrianna."

Shaniqua shook Fabrianna's hand while thinking she was cute too, but she didn't want to tell her that. Fabrianna was about the same height as Shaniqua, which put her at 5'2".

"We should keep in touch," Fabrianna said with a

smile, even though her deep-set, brown eyes were serious. "Give me your number and let's get together and hang out sometime."

Shaniqua nodded. She didn't see any real harm in it. The girl was very nice and was probably popular at another school.

Fabrianna changed clothes and met Shaniqua at the cash register where Fabrianna jotted her number down. "So can I have yours, too?"

Shaniqua hesitated for a moment, and then jotted her cell number down on an old clothing receipt.

Chapter 3

Friday morning, Natasha awoke early, so early the sky was still black and the house chilled. The clock showed 3:45. She had awakened with the same queasy feeling that she went to bed with. She curled into a fetal position and wrapped her arms around her legs. In thirteen hours, she would be on a huge plane bound for Paris. She tried to focus on all the fun she was going to have, but even that didn't alleviate the unsettled stomach. She jumped out of bed, clicked on the nightlight and began rummaging through her luggage.

"Tasha, what on earth are you doing up?"

Natasha jumped, startled to see her mother in the doorway. "I can't sleep."

"Well, you need to try. It's going to take nine hours flying nonstop to get to Paris."

"I know, don't remind me," she said, plunking down on the edge of her bed. "Mom, what if I get claustrophobic or worse, sick from breathing in everyone's disgusting germs?"

Natasha's mother took a seat beside her daughter.

"Sweet pea, you'll do fine. Don't worry. That plane is so big, you're going to forget you're on it." Ms. Harris gently cupped her daughter's chin. "Now relax. Look forward to it. It's going to be a great experience. You get to use your French and you'll have your best friend Brittany there."

Natasha looked up with watery eyes. "Mom, I'm going to miss you. I've never been away from you and Dad, especially for ten days."

Ms. Harris chuckled. "Natasha Elaine Harris, I know this is not my big girl acting like a baby."

Tasha pulled away quickly. "Never mind, just forget it. Will you leave, please? I'm ready to go to sleep now."

"Sweet pea, I'm sorry. I didn't mean it like that. I'm just not used to you being afraid to do anything. Tasha, you've always been fearless since the day you were born. I remember when you were six months old and you were trying to walk, yet you couldn't even sit up good by yourself. But you wanted to keep up with Nate," her mother said, chuckling.

Natasha focused on the floor, refusing to make eye contact.

"Mommy has always been proud of you and your accomplishments. You're the first person in this family to ever visit another country. Natasha, that's no small accomplishment. You're about to do what many folks wish they could do. This is an opportunity of a lifetime." Ms. Harris drew in a deep breath. "Sweetheart, I know you'll be fine. You'll forget all about the size of the plane. You might even forget about us back home!"

Natasha grinned and wiped her eyes. "Thanks, Mom."

"Is Stephen still coming to the airport with us?"

Natasha shook her head. "I don't want him to."

"Why not?"

"Because I just don't. I want to be with my family."

Ms. Harris stood up. "Okay, sweet pea. Well, if you change your mind, we're leaving the house at 1:30 p.m. Try to get some sleep. Good night."

As soon as her mother closed the door, Natasha picked up the black cordless phone next to her bed and dialed Stephen's cell number. What she had to say couldn't wait another day. The phone rang several times before going to voicemail. She hung up, then turned off her nightlight and began counting the savory croissants she would soon enjoy in Paris.

Hartsfield International Airport was one of the busiest airports in the world. Brittany could navigate through the humongous terminal with the ease of an Atlanta-based flight attendant. She had flown at least ten times a year, so her parents' assistance was neither welcome nor needed. Her dad stalled the car in front of the outdoor ticket counter while her mom was in the passenger seat running down the checklist.

Brittany sucked her teeth and rolled her eyes. "Mom, please quit worrying. I have everything I need, passport, driver's license. The only thing I'm missing is money."

Her dad turned around to face her, cleared his throat and then dug inside the pocket of his blazer and pulled out a white envelope. A huge smile spread across Brittany's face, her dimples were break-dancing on her cheeks. She was taking two practically empty suitcases to save room for all of the new clothes she was going to bring home. Peeking inside the envelope, she quickly counted the money. "Five hundred dollars! What am I suppose to do with that? That's nothing; I can't buy anything with that."

Her mom offered an apologetic smile. "Brittany, your dad—look that's all that we have to spare."

"Where's the credit card you always let me use?"

Mrs. Brown looked to her husband. "Honey, I think she should have it in case of an emergency."

Her dad dug in his pocket for his wallet and whipped out a platinum Visa. "But only for emergency. It's not to be used for frivolous stuff, Brittany!"

Brittany flashed her infamous smirk, thinking what her lips were unwilling to say, "Whatever." She grabbed the door lever, rammed her body against the car door for dramatic effect and then slammed the door of her dad's Mercedes Benz closed. "This is going to be a lousy trip. I wish I wasn't even going!" She stormed around to the trunk of the car and began shoving all her items into the largest Louis Vuitton suitcase.

Her mother followed her. "What are you doing?"

"Nothing." Brittany said, choking back tears. "What's the point of taking two empty suitcases; I don't have any money to buy anything."

"Brittany, your dad's going through a rough patch right now with work and we need you to be understanding. This isn't easy for me either."

"Whatever." Brittany barely hugged her parents goodbye and went searching for the group. Her mind was on shopping. Clothes were expensive in the fashion capital of the world; she would barely be able to afford one decent outfit.

Madame Knight, the French teacher, gathered the twenty-two students and paired everyone together. Natasha was relieved that Brittany, the seasoned traveler, was her partner. Natasha was busy studying the 757 Delta plane parked at the gate. It was big, but it didn't look big enough to hold everyone waiting in the gate area, she thought. *What if it suddenly fell out of the sky?* Natasha quickly changed her thoughts and began watching Brittany with a credit card in hand trying to get the customer service representative to upgrade them to first class. Brittany had said that first class had the best food, all her favorites: filet mignon, fancy salads, warm nuts and cookies, pizza and ice cream sundaes. Brittany sashayed her way back over to the group with her Dolce & Gabana shades perched on top of her head. "Tasha, I tried, but he said it was a full flight and they would not be able to accommodate any upgrades. Can you believe that? That's pathetic!"

"Girl, it's okay. We're straight," Natasha said, walking over to board the plane. She desperately wanted to tell someone how her nerves were in her stomach. She handed the gate agent her ticket and walked down the long corridor. The plane's doorway was entirely too small; she felt the need to duck her head as she stepped into the plane. Flight attendants, wearing their customary cheesy grins, directed her to her seat all the way at the rear of the aircraft. Natasha took a seat in front of the aft lavatory.

Brittany followed. "Oh, heck no, I am not going to sit here and listen to the toilet flush for nine hours. That thing sounds like a gigantic vacuum pump." She waved a flight attendant over. "Excuse me, but can we please switch seats?"

The flight attendant offered an indifferent grin. "Sorry, it's a full flight."

Brittany looked at the attendant's nametag on her navy blue dress and smiled sweetly, letting her dimples do all the charming. "Please, Ms. Stacey, see what you can do?"

"I wish there was something I could do, but the flight's full. You can always ask a passenger if they'd be willing to switch with you."

Brittany petulantly plunked down in the seat and whispered rather loudly to Natasha, "Fine. I guess it's me, you and the freakin' toilet!" She whipped out her cell phone and began telling her mother their ordeal. "But you guys could have paid the extra money. Jeez! We never rode in coach over to France." After minutes of silence, Brittany flipped her phone closed and tried to relax in the tight seat. But comfort and coach just didn't go together. "Ugh!"

Natasha steadied her nerves by snacking on Twizzlers and watching the baggage handlers toss luggage into the underbelly of the plane. She hoped her luggage was going to make it. It would be awful to be stuck in Paris without clothes. Her mind traveled to Stephen. She had succeeded in dodging his phone calls all day because she didn't want him tagging along to the airport. She didn't want to tell her friends, but she felt like Stephen was ready to take their relationship to the next level. All he talked about was prom night and going to college together. Natasha closed her eyes and tried to block their previous conversation out, but the words just kept whipping around in her mind like a fierce tornado. "Tasha, you know I care for you. I'm not like those other guys, but I do have needs. I want my first time to be with you, someone I love."

Suddenly, Natasha felt the plane slowly pushing back from the gate. The palms of her hands grew sweaty. She clasped her hands together, letting her fingers console one another. They sat on the runway nearly thirty minutes before their plane was cleared for take-off. Cold sweat stood out on her brow while she consumed the last piece of comfort, her red licorice. The anticipation was killing her. A series of chimes sounded and then the captain's voice reverberated over the intercom. "Flight attendants, prepare the cabin for take-off."

Minutes later, the plane took off full speed down the

runway. Natasha reached for Brittany's arm. Her heart was pounding. All of Atlanta was passing by so fast. She closed her eyes. When the cranking of the wheels buckled underneath, the plane went soaring through the sky, but her stomach felt as though it had been abandoned on the tarmac. As the plane climbed to an altitude of 35,000 feet, Natasha peeked out of the window at the diminishing city. The houses were getting smaller and smaller. Swimming pools resembled little blue puddles. Atlanta looked so different from up above.

Suddenly the plane dropped like it was falling out of the sky. Natasha let out a high-pitched squeal and grabbed Brittany's arm. Everyone in the back of the plane turned to look; some chuckled, while others snubbed her. Three tones chimed. Seconds later, the pilot came on over the intercom. "Good afternoon folks, this is Captain Dacosta. We're going to keep the seatbelt sign on a little longer due to turbulence. Once the turbulence has subsided, the flight attendants will be serving dinner and drinks. So, please sit back and enjoy the flight. Once again, welcome aboard." Natasha looked at Brittany through watery eyes and held her hand. Brittany patted her friend's hand but all she could think about was how she was going to fill up her empty suitcase.

Chapter 4

Shaniqua's hands were submerged in soapy dishwater when the phone rang. "I got it, Granny," she said, drying her hands on a watermelon-decorated dishcloth. The sleek white cordless was nearly lost in the sea of fruits plastered against the kitchen wall. She had offered to buy her grandmother new wallpaper, but Granny refused it. Her grandmother loved that the wallpaper matched the throw rugs, hand towels and magnets on the refrigerator.

"Hello."

"Hello, is Shaniqua there?"

"It's me. Who is this?"

"This is Fabrianna. We met at the store last week."

Shaniqua frowned to help jar her memory. A second later, it clicked—the semi weird chick with the piercing under her lip. "Oh, hey, what's up?"

"What are you doing tonight?"

"Nothing."

"You want to catch a movie at Stonecrest?"

"I guess." The words tumbled out. It wasn't like she had anyone else to hang with. Brittany and Natasha were in Paris and cousin Nee Nee was working at the club as usual.

"Cool. Where do you live? I'll come scoop you."

Shaniqua gave the directions and then hurried to her bedroom—her favorite room in their two-bedroom townhouse. With the money she made over the summer, she bought a bed in a bag set. A luxurious brown and powder blue comforter with matching throw pillows spruced up her once drab bedroom. She hardly noticed anymore that she didn't have a headboard. Posters of Lil Kim, Chris Brown, Bow Wow and Ciara added a little flair to her eggshell colored walls, but not enough; she still wanted to paint the room baby blue.

A tiny bit of excitement fueled Shaniqua as she searched her closet for a cute outfit. The only people that she ever hung out with were her best friends and occasionally her cousin. But she hardly saw her cousin since they worked different schedules and Nee Nee no longer lived down the street. She had her own pad in Decatur. Shaniqua loved being over there because Nee Nee kept her pantry stocked with chips, cookies, candies and soda. All the things she loved, but her grandmother never bought because Granny always said, "Junk food costs too much. I can make you somethin' for cheaper and it'll be better for ya'." Her grandmother never seemed to understand her hamburgers and fries weren't like McDonald's, no matter how good a cook she was. The burger was always two inches thick and the fries were twice the size of Shaniqua's index finger.

She showered and dressed in dark rinse skinny jeans and a yellow-green top with apple green stilettos.

Working at the store had its perks; she purchased the latest fashions before anyone else had them plus receive the employee discount. When she finished dressing, she made her way downstairs where her grandmother was watching T.D. Jakes on television. "Granny, I'm going to the movies with a friend."

"What friend?"

"Oh, you don't know her. I met her at the mall a few days ago. Her name's Fabrianna. She's pretty cool."

Her grandmother peered over the rim of her glasses, the tarnished gold chain dangling at the sides of her face. "Well, I like ta meet her."

Her eyes immediately stole over to her grandmother's now fully white hair sprouting wildly. "Yes, ma'am," Shaniqua said, making a mad dash back to her bedroom for the comb and brush. She had spoiled her grandmother rotten. Most days Granny's hair remained uncombed unless Shaniqua took the time to comb it. Saturday nights had been the designated beauty parlor night since she started doing her grandmother's hair at age ten. She would wash it and then rake the piping hot pressing comb through it, letting the heat mix with the green grease, emitting a sweet oil smell. "Fried, dyed and laid to the side, fresh for the Lawd's day," Granny would say.

When Fabrianna pulled up outside their townhouse, Shaniqua studied her from the doorway. Fabrianna looked so different than she remembered. Baggy jeans and an oversized Sixers' throwback jersey consumed her petite frame. Her hips were straight like a boy's and her chest was like that of a pre-teen. Her hair was braided neatly in cornrows straight to the back, revealing a chiseled bone structure. "What's up, Fabrianna?" she said, holding the door open. "Dang girl, you look so different."

The very noticeable piercing underneath Fabrianna's bottom lip greeted Shaniqua. "What's up?"

"My grandmoms wants to meet you," Shaniqua said, her mind racing back to her grandmother's teeth. She wondered if they were in her mouth or in the glass jar on the coffee table, as usual. Shaniqua cautiously walked Fabrianna into the living room where she took a seat on the new tan sofa. Red and orange throw pillows shifted as they sat down. She was glad that she straightened the house. Granny had trained her well. "Don't matter how big or how small a person's house, cleanliness is next to Godliness." Shaniqua looked at the empty glass jar on the table. "Granny, this is Fabrianna."

Her grandmother revealed the coffee-stained porcelain in her mouth. "Hi baby, how you?" she said, extending her dark, wrinkled hand. She held Fabrianna's hand for a second or two, discreetly studying it. To some people, the human hand is as revealing as the face in expressing temperament, heredity and life habits.

"Good."

"You go to school with Shaniqua?"

29

"No, ma'am."

"What's that thing in yo' mouth? Shaniqua, is that the same thing that Renee got in her mouth?"

Shaniqua glanced at the shiny silver hoop protruding from Fabrianna's chin. "Yes, ma'am."

"Girl, what's wrong with you?" Granny said, frowning at Fabrianna. "You some kinda street woman or somethin'?"

Fabrianna looked embarrassed. "No, ma'am."

"What school are you?"

"I go to a Catholic school."

"Oh, I see." Granny offered a slightly pleasing nod to her granddaughter, then took a moment to collect her thoughts. "Well, y'all be careful out there. There's lots of devilment in the streets and everything that glitters ain't gold."

Shaniqua kissed her grandmother goodbye and followed Fabrianna to her car, a new Mitsubishi Eclipse. "Girl, this is tzight!"

"Thanks. Got it last year when I turned sixteen."

Shaniqua thought of Brittany. There wasn't any room in her life for another spoiled, rich chick.

"You don't look anything like your grandmother. Where's your mother?"

Shaniqua ogled the faded hot pink polish on her toenails. She knew the question was coming. It always came. Why were other kids so curious about her mother? She wasn't even that concerned about her. Karen could stay in whatever hellhole she was in, she thought, especially after their fight last year when her mother had stolen their rent money. Whenever people looked at her and then at her grandmother; they failed to hide their thoughts. Their facial expression showed that they assumed she was adopted because she bore none of the Williams' trademark features—very dark skin, plump, wide noses and full lips. Her own lips were very thin. Her skin was so light she could almost pass for white, except the bushiness of her hair when it wasn't braided would give it away. For that reason, she kept her hair in micros, to enhance her ethnicity in case people wanted to question it. Shaniqua fiddled with her fingers under the weight of Fabrianna's heavy stare. She had no intention of telling a complete stranger about her personal business. "My mom's away doing her thing."

"Oh for real, like what?"

Shaniqua's eyebrows puckered in the center of her forehead and offered her new friend an unpleasant look that ended the conversation. Fabrianna cranked up the rap music. The base was throbbing as they rolled down Covington Highway, turning heads left and right. Two fine chicks kickin' it is what everyone had to be thinking. Shaniqua's micro braids blew in the wind like strings from a kite on a gusty day. Fabrianna did a couple of krump moves while driving like she could really krump. Fabrianna was definitely not another Brittany. In some ways, she had a rough disposition, almost like a thuggish boy. But judging from the car that she was driving, Shaniqua knew that she hadn't been raised in a ghetto. The closest Fabrianna probably ever came to the ghetto was picking her up in front of her house.

The theater was packed as usual with teenagers. In Atlanta, there were only a few hangouts for teens: the movies, Lenox Mall and Atlantic Station. Fabrianna whipped the car into a space at the far end of the parking lot. Shaniqua was busy admiring herself in the mirror and reapplying lip gloss when Fabrianna nudged her. "Yo', hand me my piece down there," she said, pointing on the floor of the passenger seat.

Shaniqua frowned. "Hand you what?"

"My piece, my gun."

"What? Girl, are you crazy? Why do you have that thing?"

"I don't go anywhere without it."

"Are you in a gang or something?" Shaniqua scanned the parking lot. "Is somebody after you?"

Fabrianna's voice wasn't husky, but it seemed like she was trying to make it sound tough and deep. "Naw, everything's straight. I just don't go anywhere without it. I like to keep myself protected at all times."

Shaniqua studied Fabrianna, trying to read her. One minute, she sounded and acted like a privileged princess and then the next she was trying to be a thug. "Protected from what, 'cause I don't need no drama in my life."

"Shaniqua," Fabrianna's voice softened. "Relax, it's

not what you're thinking. I'm not beefing with nobody."

The silence was deafening.

"Everything's cool, I promise. I'll tell you about it at another time."

Shaniqua studied Fabrianna who was wearing a pleasant look on her face, but her eyes were sad, almost vacant like she wasn't really in the moment. Something was definitely up with her, but Shaniqua couldn't put her finger on it. She heard the sincerity in her new friend's voice and opened the car door. "Well, I'm not touching it. I don't want my fingerprints on it."

When they reached the movie theater, Fabrianna stepped up to the window and paid for the tickets.

"Girl, you don't have to pay my way in. I got money."

Fabrianna smiled. "I want to."

The girls made their way inside and enjoyed the movie. When it was over, they decided to get something to eat. "Let's go down to Little Five Points," Fabrianna said.

"Why you want to go way down there? Weirdos, gothics, and gays all hang out there."

"There's a cool spot where a lot of my friends hang out."

Shaniqua looked around the bare looking restaurant where they took a seat in a wooden booth. She studied the menu. "Girl, what is this?"

"I'm a vegetarian."

Shaniqua's face twisted into a weird expression. "Vegetarian. Why you want to be a vegetarian?"

"Do you really want to know?" Fabrianna shook her head. "No, you don't."

"Yes, I do."

"All right, let me break it down to you. See, it's like this, I gave up meat three years ago when I was a freshman. But, I'm not what you would call a vegan. Vegans won't eat any dairy products, eggs or honey. I eat some dairy products, I just don't eat meat."

"What's wrong with meat?"

"I just don't like what they do to the meat."

"That's 'cause you ain't had Granny's pork chops." Shaniqua looked at the menu. "Well, if this is a vegetarian restaurant, how in the world is a hot dog not meat?"

"They make it with tofu."

"Tofu, fufu, girl, please," Shaniqua said, sucking on her front teeth as if she were sucking out a piece of fried pork chop. "Give me a hot dog with some pork or beef, or something."

"Just try it."

When their food arrived, Shaniqua studied the hot dog. It looked the same. She raised it to her mouth, but decided to smell it first. "Well, it smells alright. I guess it ain't going to kill me."

"No, this ain't going to kill you," Fabrianna said with a laugh. "But the other stuff will."

Shaniqua took a bite and swallowed hard like she used to when Granny would force her to eat liver.

Shaniqua and Fabrianna talked briefly about their families and then about graduation night. "I'm going into the military," Fabrianna announced.

"Why?"

"Because my parents are really pushing college down my throat and I'm not ready. I want to travel and see the world first. The day after graduation, I'm out! I can't stand living at home with them."

Shaniqua shrugged. She wasn't trying to get too personal because she didn't want anyone asking her questions about her family life. The next question was bound to be, "Where's your dad?" She hated saying, "I don't know him, never met him." It was easier to avoid the topic altogether. She had grown tired of lying like she used to when she was in elementary school. "I thought about going to college. But we ain't got—I mean, we don't have the money for college. So I think I'm going to work for awhile, stack dough."

"You'd be perfect for the military."

"Me?"

"Yes, you could travel the world and they'll give you

money to go to school as soon as you finish."

"Girl, please, I ain't trying to fight in nobody's war."

"Well, what if everyone thought like that, then we wouldn't be enjoying the liberties that we do now."

"True that," Shaniqua said rolling her eyes. "But I'm not worried about everybody. I'm thinking about me and my grandmother. I couldn't leave her. She's my heart."

They had just about finished eating when Fabrianna got a phone call. She grabbed the check. "My friends can't make it. You ready to ride out?"

A waiter with dreadlocks sprawled down his back grabbed the money and the bill that Fabrianna sat on the table. "Girl, you don't have to keep paying my way in everything," Shaniqua said.

"It's cool, I asked you out."

The words sat in her stomach like food that was ready to be regurgitated. Something just wasn't sitting right. She hated to question why Fabrianna was being so nice and making her feel special. Next to Natasha, this was the nicest anyone had ever treated her. It was fun, but different than being with Natasha and Brittany.

"You want to walk next door and get tattoos?"

Shaniqua's eyes lit up. Her cousin Nee Nee had been promising to take her for months. "Girl, I already know which one I want. I hope they have it at this shop," she said, following Fabrianna inside the cramped parlor.

Shaniqua quickly picked out a colorful butterfly, while Fabrianna combed the wall looking for something. "Girl, I'm scared, but I'm ready. I'm getting it on the small of my back so my grandmother won't see it."

"So, who's first?" said the heavyset tattoo artist.

"I am." Shaniqua jumped in front of the man. "Is this going to hurt?"

"The only thing I can say is, it depends on your threshold for pain."

Shaniqua glanced at his thick forearm completely covered with tattoos. Her thoughts raced to Nee Nee's back. She had six. Shaniqua drew in a deep breath and exhaled noisily. "Alright, let's do this, Brutis." The tiny needle pressed into the pores of her skin. "Nooo!" She bit into her bottom lip to numb the pain.

Chapter 5

After a day's rest in the hotel, Brittany and Natasha were finally over jet lag. Paris, France was seven hours ahead of the Eastern Standard time zone. Brittany awoke and observed their surroundings with mild irritation. Their hotel room was nearly the size of her bedroom closet at home. There was no space for luxury items, only the bare necessities could fit. It resembled a college dorm room more than a hotel. Mounted in one corner was a television set small enough to fit comfortably in a dollhouse. Twin beds were only a few feet apart while a little wooden chair held the corner. A slight smile crept across Brittany's face—at least it was clean and most of all, her parents weren't there.

After the girls showered and dressed, they met their group in the hotel's cafeteria for breakfast. They were in line when they heard a commotion. "Yo' man, where the bacon, eggs and pancakes?" Alex, a redhead pimply face boy, asked. Everyone laughed. Alex was always trying to turn the French language into American slang.

Brittany twisted her mouth into a scowl. "Alex, the

French do not eat heavy for breakfast. Hence, le petite déjeuner!" she said, grabbing a baguette.

"Can a brotha at least get some French toast?"

Everyone laughed. Brittany rolled her eyes. "Alex, I know you think you are a brother, but somebody forgot to tell you, you're not! And somebody also forgot to tell you that French toast didn't originate in France. Duhhh!"

Moans and groans erupted from the crowd indicating that Brittany had won. Madame Knight glared at her students with displeasure. "Settle down everyone; bon appetite."

Natasha placed a fluffy, quarter-moon shaped croissant on her plate and took a seat. The plane ride was definitely worth an authentic French croissant, she thought as she bit into the rich, flaky pastry.

After a quick breakfast, the group made their way through the city of Paris, the most popular tourist destination in the world, by riding the Metro. There was so much to see. Rows of apartment buildings lined the narrow streets, classic French Citroen cars were packed in tightly against one another, creating constant traffic jams.

When the group arrived at the Louvre, the most famous museum in the world, the line to gain entry was down the block. Sprawling over several city blocks, the museum's neo-classical architecture framed the skyline while a large glass replica of an Egyptian pyramid, surrounded by three smaller ones, decorated the main courtyard.

"Jeez, we're going to spend our whole day waiting in line," Brittany pouted. "I'd rather go shopping."

"Patience, si'l vous plait," Madame Knight said.

Thirty minutes later, the group was browsing through the halls of The Louvre. Natasha's thoughts were of Stephen. A small part of her wished that he were there to enjoy it. He loved museums. They loved museums together. Sophomore year on their school field trip to the High Museum of Art in Atlanta is where their friendship took root and sprouted into a relationship.

A huge crowd swarmed the Mona Lisa. Brittany and Natasha made there way to the front. Brittany studied the portrait for a while. "What's the big deal?"

"Shhh!" Natasha glanced around to see if anyone was witnessing her friend's ignorance.

Then, a tall, burly man with an American southern drawl interrupted. "Yeah, I don't see it either," he said, then bellowed out a deep snort for a laugh.

Natasha offered an apologetic smile. He seemed too far removed from even American culture to attempt to explain the significance of the Mona Lisa. Natasha studied the portrait. For some reason she always assumed it was larger. Her thoughts skipped over to Stephen. He would be so happy to witness this painting. She made a mental note to buy him a copy of the picture. Maybe not, she thought, he might be insulted by a print.

Maybe she would find him a nice painting on the streets. France was known for cultivating fine artists. All the greats like Manet, Renoir and Delacrois had spent time perfecting their craft on the streets of Paris.

Brittany scrunched her face. "It just looks like some painting of a white woman."

Natasha glared at her friend. "If Stephen was here, he could break it down better, but I'll do my best. The reason why this piece is so great is because Leonardo da Vinci used some really innovative techniques like Sfumato. See the hazy, soft-focus effect? He also used the chiaroscuro technique to create the light and shadow you see."

"Great, thank you, Professor Harris," Brittany said with a smirk. "I'll store that away in my memory bag of minutia."

"And a lot of people like the mysterious look on the model's face. I'm surprised your parents hadn't brought you here before."

"They have. I didn't see the significance of it then and still don't. Let's go on to something else."

They coursed the massive maze of the museum, exploring various exhibitions. They were studying Oriental antiques as a little Frenchman was staring at Natasha.

"Dang, Tasha, you pulling the Frenchies, too! I guess it's true what they say about French dudes liking the sistas. Go on hot, momma," Brittany squealed.

"Shut up, Brit!" Natasha looked over casually at the man who wore a weird, eager expression on his face. "Let's go, girl."

Brittany and Natasha eased away and went into another section of antiques. Natasha turned around to make sure he wasn't following them. "Girl, whatever you do, do not turn around."

Brittany whipped her head around to look at him. Her smile quickly faded. He was just a few feet away from them. She grabbed her best friend's arm. "Tasha, I'm scared. What are we going to do?"

"We have to find a security guard."

They both scanned the area for help, but it was so crowded they couldn't find anyone. The well-dressed man in a cheap smile slowly approached them. He was a typical Frenchman, slender build and average height. "Excusez-moi, Mademoiselle," the stranger said. "Vous ete tres belle. Est-ce-que vous ete une model?"

Natasha blushed. "Yes."

"Ahhh, American. Very good," he said. His accent was thick as if his tongue was cemented in his mouth. "Who do you model for?"

"Well, I don't model for anyone right now. I'm a senior in high school."

"You must come to Paris to model. You have great look. I am an agent. I book models for fashion shows. Take my card, and if you are interested when you finish high school, you contact me. Yes?"

Natasha took his business card and nodded. Her voice had been temporarily silenced by her nerves.

"You very exotic. You do very well in the European market. You make lots of money. Au revoir, Mademoiselles."

"Au revoir," Brittany called out after him. Then she turned to Natasha. "Ohmigod, Tasha, he wants to hire you! I wonder if he's for real. You know they have a lot of scams with that modeling thing. Girl, they could sell you into the sex trade or something. They could—"

Natasha tuned her friend out and after studying the business card, said, "Brit, I think he's for real. Paris Models, Inc. is very reputable. Ohmigod, what am I going to tell my parents? I really want to do this."

A frown sat on Brittany's face as if she was sucking on a lemon. "So you aren't going to college?"

"Girl, this is the chance of a lifetime."

For the remainder of the museum visit, Natasha carried herself the way her modeling instructors encourage. "Head up, shoulders back and lift your thighs when you walk," Ms. Isabella would say. There was no telling who else she might meet. There were scores of rumors of models being discovered on the streets, in airports, restaurants, but Natasha never thought in a million years that it would happen to her in a museum.

The following day, the group walked the café-lined streets of Paris. The Champs-Élysées, one of the many tourist attractions and a major shopping street of Paris, was crowded with people. The avenue has been called "la plus belle avenue du monde" (the most beautiful avenue in the world). Everyone looked chic, from the elderly to newborn babies. It made Brittany feel at home to see people who cared for clothes. In the States, it bothered her, as well as her mother, to see people dressed as if they had been working in the cotton fields all day. Her mother always said, "Dress up and you'll feel better. No matter what the situation." Truth is she was feeling a little jealous about Natasha's good fortune. Brittany wondered why nothing big ever happened to her. She had been to Paris twice a year for the past ten years, and no one ever stopped her on the street.

Taking her mother's advice, she grabbed Natasha's arm and dipped into the first boutique that she came to. Her frustrations would be no more. It was time for a new summer wardrobe. Her eyes immediately found a gorgeous, white halter-top sundress. She grabbed her size and darted into the dressing room. The dress was a perfect fit. She had to have it. She made her way to the checkout counter to a thin blond woman with badly stained teeth. "Allo, is this it for you?"

Brittany always wondered how the French could tell that she was American. She hadn't said a word. "Yes."

"That will be five hundred sixty-nine dollars," the woman said politely.

Brittany's dad's voice ricocheted between her ears, "Only for emergency." She scanned the small boutique for Natasha who was busy orchestrating posing techniques in the mirror. She whipped out her dad's credit card and handed it to the woman. *Definitely an emergency!* She grabbed her bag and proceeded to the next store in search of matching shoes, a handbag, and jewelry.

Chapter 6

Sunday afternoon, on the ride home from the airport, Natasha told her mom all about the trip—the view from the top of the Eiffel tower, the parks and fountains, the stained glass windows of the Notre Dame Cathedral. And of course, the fabulous cafes they dined in and the outfits she had bought. She even brought her mother back a brown and black faux fur scarf, which she and Brittany had had a heated discussion about. Brittany didn't see anything wrong with fur. Her justification was that her mom had several fur coats in varying lengths and styles. Natasha argued that it wasn't right to kill an innocent animal for human luxury. She wasn't sure how her mom would feel about faux fur, hopefully she would like the scarf just the same. But the best news of all, she would save—save until the time was right.

When Natasha arrived home, jet lag consumed her, but she had to see Stephen. The time apart had been good. People always said, "Absence makes the heart grow fonder." She showered and changed into a comfortable pink and green warm-up. Though she planned to pledge

Delta like her mom, she still loved to wear green. The doorbell rang, catapulting her into chaos. Stephen arrived much earlier than she anticipated. He must have missed her too, she thought. She slicked her hair back into a low ponytail and rushed downstairs, taking two at a time.

She swung open the door and fell into Stephen's arms like a scripted scene from a romantic comedy. Their mouths met in a quick kiss. She didn't want her mom or Neil to see them. Natasha escorted him into the family room where Neil was playing a video game. She cleared her throat to signal Neil to leave. Neil, a freshman at Miller Grove High School, politely ignored his sister's cue. Neil had made the varsity basketball squad his freshman year, so he thought that gave him carte blanche to everything. Not. "Neil?"

"What?"

"I have company."

"So."

She sprinted upstairs and complained to their mother. Moments later, Ms. Harris called down the stairs for Neil. Natasha returned to the room with a smirk on her face while Neil packed up the game and slid it back into the credenza.

Stephen took a seat on the sofa. "So how was the trip?" There was no excitement in his voice.

"It was fabulous. I'm sorry I didn't get a chance to e-mail you as promised. But we stayed so busy. They kept us on a strict schedule."

Stephen nodded.

Natasha stared at him. He looked good. His hair was neatly twisted and hung right beside his ears. She slid her body into his. The smell of his after-shave was intoxicating. "I brought you something," she said, digging into her bag and whipping out an elaborate set of paintbrushes.

His face lit up like a child's on Christmas morning. "Wow! Tasha, this is awesome," he said, staring at the deluxe set of brushes. "I can't believe you bought me this. They don't even sell these brushes in the States. Thank you. But, you shouldn't have."

"I wanted to. And look what else I have for you?" She whipped around from the side of the sofa, an 11" x 17" portrait of the Eiffel Tower. "Can you see me? I had the artist sketch me standing directly in front of it. Isn't that cool? I want you to always remember me."

Stephen's expression turned cold. "Why? Are you going somewhere?"

Natasha looked at him curiously. Comments like this were beginning to irk her. Rather than get into a fight, she would choose peace. Her mind combed over topics to discuss. She thought of telling Stephen about the modeling thing, but she wanted to wait and tell everyone when she had more information. An uncomfortable silence loomed in the air.

Suddenly with a mischievous grin twisted on his face, Stephen reached for his girlfriend's hand. "So what are we going to do after the prom?"

Natasha drew in a deep breath and exhaled. "Jeez, I don't even have my prom dress yet."

"You don't sound like you're that interested."

Natasha turned on the TV in an attempt to divert the conversation. Everyone was talking about the senior prom. She thought she would have been excited to attend, but it was creating feelings of anxiety. Everyone was saying what they were going to do afterwards, and almost all the kids were getting hotel rooms. Some hotels were even offering high school students discounts on the room rates.

"It'll be fun, I promise. Do you at least know what color you want us to wear?"

"Nope." Natasha rubbed her eyes, unaware of her mascara. The jet lag had returned sooner than she expected. "Stephen, is it okay if we catch up tomorrow, I'm really sleepy."

"Oh, sure, babe, no problem."

Natasha walked him to the door, gave him a quick kiss goodbye.

Chapter 7

When Brittany's mom picked her up at the airport, Brittany immediately sensed that something was eating away at her mother. Her mouth was twitching non-stop, the way it had several years ago when her parents were on the brink of divorce. At the time, Brittany was only thirteen, but she remembered her mother's lips twitching uncontrollably as she shoved pots and pans around the kitchen in an effort to make dinner. An awful, empty feeling crowded Brittany's stomach as she sat in the passenger seat, thinking and growing angrier by the street. A divorce. How could they do this to her? They could have at least waited until she was out of high school. A divorce. That would explain why they were being so tight with money. Tears brimmed in her eyes as she watched her mother gripping the steering wheel of her Lexus. Her parents had been her entire world. Why did they have to get a divorce right now? Everything seemed to be going fine. Her dad was working a lot more than usual. Maybe that was his way of dealing with it, she thought. They had no right to take their problems out on her.

"So how was your trip?" Brittany's mother asked.

Brittany blinked back the mounting tears and disguised the hurt in her voice with attitude. "Boring. I couldn't shop. I didn't have any money."

Her mother cast a curious glance at Brittany, then checked her rear-view mirror. "We need to talk."

She offered her mother an indignant look that said what her mouth would not, "Talk!"

"I hate to be the one to tell you this, but some things are going to change around here."

Brittany pursed her lips and rolled her eyes, bracing herself, her heart. To mask the pain that she was feeling, she tuned her mother out and focused on getting home so she could check her MyPage messages. Hopefully, Dante had sent her an e-mail.

"Young lady, are you listening to me?"

"How can I not? I'm sitting in the car next to you, aren't I?"

"You watch your tone. I know you're upset about your shopping money, but that was beyond our control."

Brittany folded her arms across her chest as if she was ready to do battle. Without warning, tears surfaced again. "Why do I have to suffer just because you and daddy are getting a divorce?" She tried desperately not to blink her tears down. "That's not fair. All you had to do was go to the bank and get more money like you always do. What's the big deal, God!"

Brittany's mother looked at her daughter indignantly, shaking her head. "Your father and I are not getting a divorce."

Brittany whipped her head around to face her

mother. Long, loose curls followed. Her voice softened. "You're not?"

"No, we're not. Where on earth did you get that idea?"

"The last time I seen you this upset, you guys were going to get one."

"It's because I have something to tell you and I don't think you are going to like it."

"Well, at least you're not getting a divorce, so I can handle it. What is it?"

Brittany's mom looked at her, then back to the road. "I don't have an easy way to say this, but your car went back."

"Went back where?"

"Back to the dealership."

"When can we pick it up?"

"We can't."

"What!" Brittany fumed. "Who wrecked my car? Why'd you let Kevin drive it while I was gone? Jeez!"

"Brittany?"

"How bad is it?"

"Brittany?"

"He's going to pay to fix every last scratch on my car. I am not playing. He had no business—"

"Brittany! That's not what happened."

Defiant, she folded her arms across her chest. "Well, what happened to my car, Mom?"

"Your dad sent it back because we can't afford it right now."

She glared at her mother who was staring at the road ahead. She was trying to process it all. Did her parents really take her car back? "Mom, I don't understand what you are talking about."

"Brittany Ann, I need you to act grown up." Her mother swallowed hard. "We can no longer afford to keep paying the lease on the car. Your dad is trying to build a new clinic and we are strapped for cash. The new clinic cost a lot of money. It's going to be state of the art. It's an investment."

Brittany's large, doe eyes were filled with tears, again. "But why?"

"What do you mean why? Why what?" Her mother's voice broke into a cadence. She was obviously trying to adjust to the lifestyle change, too.

Tears cascaded down Brittany's round cheeks and meshed into her pink cotton top, creating a wet spot on her blouse. She turned her attention to the tree leaves swaying ever so gently in the soft breeze, as if they had not a care in the world, while her world was crumbling all around her.

"It's only going to be for a short while," her mother said. Brittany turned to face her, but her words of protest died in her throat. "What your father is doing is great. He's going to have his own facility. That way he won't have to keep paying the hospitals and their staff every time he has to operate. It'll be better in the long run, financially speaking."

When Brittany arrived home, she ran into her bedroom. "How could they do that?" played like a broken record in her head. She combed over every inch of the car. Did they get all of her stuff out of the car? Her iPod Touch was in the glove compartment, along with her pink Fendi shades and black D&G shades. The cell phone charger.

Notes from her friends. She hated them. Why couldn't they at least wait until school was out? For Christsakes, she only had a few more weeks to go. She hated them. College couldn't come quick enough and then she would be off to Northwestern University. Suddenly, her mind raced back to the shopping spree in Paris. She had to find away to intercept the bill. They could never find out what she had spent.

To take her mind off her problems, Brittany logged onto her laptop and began checking her messages. She was glad to see that Dante had missed her. He posted comments and sent several e-mails saying he couldn't wait for her return. She was glad that he had found her online. He understood her better than anyone she had ever known. Perfect fit, she thought. Definitely much better than Marcus's lame behind. Dante didn't do drugs. He was Catholic just like she was and came from a prominent family, too. She couldn't wait to meet him in person. If he was as cute as his picture, then it was going to be on and poppin', she thought. She proceeded to type:

What's up Dante,

Sorry I didn't contact U while I was in France. And no, I didn't meet anyone else. My trip was whack! My parents didn't give me any $$$ 2 spend. Maybe I should have taken U up on your offer. I could have really used the xtra $$$. I'm going to call U with the latest on my parents. It's 2 much 2 write. I'm so hot right now, no, not what you thinkin' boy. Seriously, I feel like crying. But I'm going 2 call U after I take a nap. I have jet lag! "B" eye candy

Chapter 8

Monday morning, Shaniqua waited in the school cafeteria for Brittany and Natasha. She couldn't wait to hear all about their trip and to tell them about her new friend, Fabrianna. "Dang, what took y'all so long?" she said, as they approached the lunch table.

Brittany plunked down first and sat a pretty gift bag in front of Shaniqua. "Here, I brought you something."

She gasped, "But I didn't give you money to buy me anything."

"Duhhh, like I think I know that already!" Brittany said, reaching down into a large bag and pulling out a cute camel colored leather jacket.

"Brit, you bought that for me? A leather jacket. Ohmigod!"

"Don't flatter yourself too much. It was off-season and on sale. I figured since I couldn't wear it, I knew your little twig behind could. So consider it an early graduation present."

"Oh, Brit, that's so sweet." Shaniqua darted around to the other side of the table and bear hugged her friend.

"You ain't so bad after all."

Brittany batted her eyelashes. "Flatter me." Then her mind raced back to the credit card bill.

"So, how was it?" Shaniqua said, looking between her two friends. "What did y'all buy? What did y'all do?"

Brittany grinned. "It was fun. But Tasha is the one with all the news. Go ahead, tell her, Tasha."

Natasha was busy enjoying a glazed donut while looking out for Stephen.

"Never mind," Brittany said. "I'll tell her."

"No, I want to tell her," Natasha retorted. "It's my news."

"Dang, will somebody just tell me what happened?"

"I met an agent over there who wants me to come back to model after graduation."

"What!" Shaniqua gasped. "Girl, get out of here!"

"I was right there," Brittany chirped. "I saw everything."

Shaniqua looked intently at her friend. "For real? So what are you going to do?"

"Well, I mentioned it to my mom briefly last night before I went to bed that I had met an agent there, but she didn't really pay it any attention. So, I'm going to gather my "intel" as my dad would say, before I approach them again. That way whatever questions they have for me, I'll have the answers in black and white, and they'll have no choice but to say yes."

"Girl, that is the bomb!" Shaniqua exclaimed.

"How was your break?" Natasha asked, not wanting to soak up all the attention. "I bet you made a lot of money." She knew Shaniqua had been a little jealous of their trip. For the last couple of weeks, every time they mentioned Paris, Shaniqua would try to change the conversation.

"Girl, please, I didn't do anything, but work and hang out a little with a new friend."

Brittany smirked. "What boy?"

Shaniqua frowned. "It wasn't a boy for your information. I met this girl name Fabrianna at work. She's straight. Check this out," Shaniqua said, showing off her tattoo.

Brittany's plump lips curled into in disdain. "Girl, why'd you get that ghetto stamp?"

"A butterfly is not a ghetto stamp."

"I don't care if it's Jesus the Christ. Tattoos are the ghetto's stamp of approval."

"Whatever, Brittany, quit hating just because you can't have one. Anywho!" Shaniqua turned her attention to Natasha. "Fabrianna took me. I think you'll like her. I invited her to hang out with us on Friday night."

"I don't need any new friends," Brittany said. "Especially ghetto-fabulous ones."

Shaniqua glared at Brittany. "Girl, please, we didn't say anything when you were running up behind Mina last year, your little hot mamacita, like her stuff didn't stink, frontin' like we were the four Musketeers!"

"I was not. Tell her, Tasha."

"My name's Bennett and I'm not in it."

"Anywho!" Shaniqua rolled her eyes. "I don't have to work Friday night and I heard Jamal's having a party? So, you know it's going to be off the chain. Y'all want to go?"

"I'm game," Natasha said. "Let me make sure Stephen's okay with it."

"Dang, Tasha, he's not your husband. He's a boy, you hear that, boy friend. Y'all acting more married than my parents."

"I know. That's what I've been trying to tell y'all. I feel like he and I are on a ball and chain. He wants us to go to college together and then get an apartment together our sophomore year, get engaged our junior year and get married after college."

"Ugh!" Brittany grimaced. "And have 2.4 children and a white picket fence."

Shaniqua rolled her eyes. "Brittany please, you just jealous cause you ain't got a man."

Brittany offered her infamous smirk. "I met somebody online for your information."

"Girl, please. Have you seen him before?"

"I saw his picture on MyPage."

"Girl, he's probably some old, creepy, baldheaded, white, fifty-year-old lunatic."

Brittany flipped a curl out of her face. "Girl, please, he's finer than anyone you've ever dated. Anywho! And we're talking about going to prom together."

"Stop using my word."

"Anywho! Natasha, there's going to be so much eye candy at school, why take sand to the beach?" Brittany said, pretending to toss her a loose curl out of her face. "So what college are you going to, Shaniqua?" she said, pronouncing every syllable.

"I didn't say I was going to college, Brittany."

"Will you guys please stop?" Natasha said, shaking

her head. "So, Shaniqua are you planning on going to the prom, too?"

"You already know, not if I don't have a date. Oh yeah, Tasha, what's up with Adonis? Is that your friends with bens?"

Natasha grinned. "Girl, please. We're just cool."

Brittany and Shaniqua exchanged knowing looks while the minutes ticked down bringing the school day to a start.

Chapter 9

Friday night, Shaniqua pranced in front of the mirror, happy that she would be the only one at the party wearing the hottest new jeans laced with pink and white rhinestones. She wasn't sure who would show up first, Brittany and Natasha or Fabrianna. She decided to go downstairs to wait for them. Granny was sitting in her favorite chair in an old housecoat that was once blue and white, but the blue had long been washed out. Shaniqua didn't care what Granny said, she was going to buy her a decent robe for Christmas this year. She had already started saving her money. Granny would have a new, plush microterry bathrobe and matching slippers, no matter the cost because Granny was worth every penny. Maybe one day she would save enough money to buy her a diamond ring or necklace, a diamond anything. Granny was too old not to have ever owned a diamond. Her wedding ring had been just a plain, thin gold band. "Hi, Granny."

Her grandmother smiled, creating a small dark hole where her teeth should have been. "Hey baby, where you off to tonight?"

"We're all going to a party."

"Girl, what you got on? I swear 'fo' God dem pants so tight, theys liable to cut off yo' blood flow."

"Granny, they're not cutting off my circulation. I promise." Shaniqua leaned down to kiss her grandmother on the forehead. She hadn't ever recalled a time in her life when she had left Granny without kissing her goodbye.

"Don't be out too late, ya' hear."

Shaniqua thought she heard Brittany's Honda pull in front of their townhouse, but it was Natasha's dad's car. She made her way over to Natasha and Brittany. "Hey y'all, I thought Brittany was driving."

"My car's in the shop getting a tune-up," Brittany blurted out. Her lie hung in the air like the stench of rotten eggs. She glanced around to see if Natasha had caught it, but she was busy on her cell.

"Stephen, it's not like that," Natasha explained. "I just want to hang with my girls a little. I understand, but we'll never have this time again. Graduation's a month away. Everybody'll be going their separate ways." Natasha rolled her eyes upward. "Fine. Whatever!" she shouted and snapped her flip phone shut.

Brittany pursed her lips. "A B See ya!"

"You ain't said nothin' slick to a can of oil!" Shaniqua said, slapping Brittany a high-five.

Natasha's brows puckered creating a deep furrow across her forehead when she stared at Shaniqua in the back seat.

"Don't mean-mug me, I didn't do it!" Shaniqua joked. "Seriously, what's wrong with you?"

"Stephen's tripping. He said that he wanted to take me to the movies tonight. And that he had a special night planned and I ruined it."

"Ohhh, you hurt his little wittle feelings. He wants to be with his lil bookie baby!"

"Shaniqua, shut up!" Natasha scolded. "You can be so antagonizing sometimes."

"You don't have to get your panties in a wad. If you that gangsta, then break up with him."

Suddenly, Fabrianna's souped-up racing engine roared down the street. Shaniqua hopped out of the car to greet her. "So, are we ready to roll?"

"Yes, get in," Fabrianna said.

"Okay, let me tell them we'll follow them to the party," Shaniqua said, and headed back to Natasha's car. "Hey, y'all, I'm going to ride with Fabrianna."

Brittany frowned. "Well, what was the point of us coming over here if we're not all riding together?"

Shaniqua shrugged. "She just said that she wanted me to ride with her."

"Well, go tell her we're all riding together," Brittany persisted.

Shaniqua went back to Fabrianna's car feeling the tug of war between friends. "They want you to ride in the car with them so that they can get a chance to holla at you."

"I don't ride with other people."

Shaniqua cupped her hands together in a playful prayer pose. "Please do it this once for me?"

Fabrianna hesitated for a moment, then finally conceded. As soon as they hopped into the back seat, Brittany turned to face Fabrianna. "Hi, I'm Brittany super-delicious-will-give-you-a-toothache-if-you-look-at-this-eye-candy-too-long Brown."

Everyone laughed. Shaniqua interrupted. "And this is my girl, Tasha."

"What's up?" Fabrianna said.

Brittany batted her eyelashes. "All right girls, let's get our party on, cause I have places to go and people to meet."

"Girl, quit tripping." Shaniqua waved her off with her hand. "What you really have to do is be back home by nine o'clock while you playin'."

"Seriously, I'm meeting my friend for the first time tonight. If y'all act right, I might let y'all meet his boys," Brittany said with mock arrogance.

"What's his name?" Shaniqua asked.

"Dante Jenkins."

Shaniqua cackled. "He sounds whack!"

"Girl, Dante is eye candy, why you playin'!" Brittany retorted. "Pretty straight white teeth. Y'all know I can't be seen with a snaggletooth Tyrese! Not! Smooth mocha brown skin. Low bald fade."

Natasha interrupted. "Brit, just don't go anywhere alone with him because you don't know him like that."

"Don't have a car, remember!" Brittany said sarcastically. Suddenly she recalled that she hadn't shared that information with them yet. Her eyes betrayed the lie. She hid her guilt behind a pompous smile. "I mean, I'm not driving tonight, duhhh!"

As the girls made their way to the party in downtown Stone Mountain, lights from Stone Mountain Park's laser show were blazing against the largest exposed rock in the world.

"Ohh, I want to see that laser show one day," Shaniqua said.

Brittany smirked. "Girl, you mean to tell me, you've been living here all your life and you haven't visited Stone Mountain?"

Quietly, Shaniqua leaned back in the seat; embarrassment marked her face.

Fabrianna turned to Shaniqua. "Girl, you're not missing anything. You can't pay me to go back there. Who wants to see them confederate fools, Robert E. Lee, Thomas "Stonewall" Jackson, and Jefferson Davis's carved images on the mountain? Segregationists put that crap up there to serve as a reminder of white supremacy. Not to mention, the Ku Klux Klan had their rebirth there in 1915. So I don't do Stone Mountain."

Shaniqua smiled. "I told y'all Fabrianna was deep."

Natasha peeked at them through the rear-view mirror. "Okay, y'all are too heavy for me."

"No, you need to know your history. If you don't know your history, it'll repeat itself." Fabrianna said. "Look at what happened with the Jena 6."

"Alright, well, we're here. Thanks for the history lesson, Fabrianna. Now, let's get our party on. My prince is waiting."

"Brittany, shut up," Natasha and Shaniqua said in unison. Laughter erupted from everyone.

Laughter was a good way to shake off one's nervousness. No one in the car admitted it, but it was always a little scary going to a party when you don't actually know the host.

Natasha had to park nearly a block away. Everyone from school said they were going to be here and from the looks of the cars stacked on both sides of the street, most of Miller Grove was in the house, Natasha thought.

With her hand in the air looking for someone to slap hands with, Shaniqua squealed. "Dang, this party is off the chain!"

"Hopefully, the cops won't shut it down," Natasha added.

Chapter 10

The dark basement was wall to wall with teens dancing and standing around in groups. The smell of marijuana greeted the girls as if it were the host of the party. Brittany's thoughts raced to her dad. He had a nose as keen as a bloodhound. If that smell got into her clothes and hair, she would be burnt toast. She wouldn't be able to see the light of day until she went off to college. Suddenly, she whipped out her phone.

"What are you doing?" Natasha asked.

"Texting Dante," she said, keying in her message. A few seconds later, her phone vibrated. "Oh, look he's here. He says he wearing a red, white and blue striped Izod."

They scanned the basement. A flashing red disco light bounced off untamed afros, weaves and braids. "It's too dark. You can't see anybody," Natasha said.

Suddenly Brittany received another text: "Meet me outside N front." Gladly, an easy excuse to get out of the funk, she thought. "Tasha, I'm going to step outside for a minute."

Brittany made her way to the front yard, but there

was no one wearing what Dante had described. Her heart was pounding with nervous energy. Brittany hoped he looked as good in person. She sauntered down to the sidewalk at the end of the yard when suddenly she felt a tap on her shoulders from behind. She spun around. It was Dante. A wave of relief washed over her that he wasn't a psycho white man who would threaten to chop her up and eat her like that cannibal Jeffrey Dahmer from Milwaukee.

"What's up, girl?" His voice was deep.

Brittany smiled while she checked him out. "Hey, what's up?" He wasn't as tall as she thought. He only had her by a few inches. She still couldn't see his features very well. A black Atlanta Braves baseball cap was snug over his head preventing her from seeing his eyes. The streetlights were spread far apart, providing little light.

"Walk with me to take my iPOD back to the car." His voice was the same monotone that it had been for the past few weeks when they had spoken over the phone. He always showed very little emotion when he spoke.

"Where's your car?"

"Just down the block here. We'll be back in like two minutes. I just don't want to lose it because I just got it." Brittany scanned the area behind him. "So, where are your boys?"

"Oh, they couldn't make it. They decided to go out with their girlfriends. I told them maybe we would meet them if you felt like it. It's up to you. They're pretty cool. I think you'll like them."

Brittany offered a casual nod while her mind processed everything. "Dang, how far down is your car?"

"Not too much further."

She looked up and down the street, and continued walking.

When they finally reached the car, Dante got in on the driver's side and slid his iPOD into the glove compartment. "So, you want to meet my friends?"

Brittany's mind raced back to Natasha. "No, I'm cool. I'll meet them next time."

"Get in. Have a seat."

Brittany hesitated for a moment and then slid into the front seat. Dante turned the car on.

"What are you doing? I'm not going anywhere."

"It's okay, I just want to cool off a little." Dante cranked up the air condition. "See."

"You seem older." A nervous chuckle escaped. "How old did you say you were?"

"Nineteen," he said, grinning.

Badly stained teeth protruded from his strong jawbone when he smiled. Brittany's thoughts raced back to the picture. She couldn't remember if he smiled in it or not. His answer ricocheted between her ears. She distinctly remembered him saying on the phone that he was eighteen, because she had commented on his deep voice.

"I really like you, Brittany."

She smiled like it hurt. An uneasy feeling was overtaking her. His car was nasty. A host of old fast food wrappers covered the floor like he hadn't cleaned the car in years. Something felt very creepy about him. Thoughts swirled in her head. She wasn't sure if it was his crooked smile, yellow teeth, bony arms, filthy car, nineteen. Her mind was swinging through the vines of thought like a monkey leaping from limb to limb in the jungle.

Dante slid closer to Brittany. She chuckled to ward of the nervousness while her mind searched for a way to lose him. She no longer wanted him at the party and definitely didn't want to introduce him to her girls.

"So, Brittany, I really like you."

Brittany wanted to smirk and say, you already said that, but instead the words, "You're cool, too," flowed out.

"You like me?"

"What?" She hid her annoyance by glancing out the window. "I just said you were cool."

"Then come closer to me."

Suddenly, the weight of reality was on her, crushing her in the seat. She had indeed seen his teeth in the picture. Perfectly straight, glistening white teeth. There was no way he could be the same person in the photograph on his MyPage page, she thought as she casually reached for the door handle. "I'm going back to the party." Without warning, he gripped her arm with extreme force and pulled her into him. Using the point of her elbow, she jammed him in his bony chest to keep him at bay. "Boy, what are you doing?"

"You're going to show me all that stuff you wrote in those e-mails." He had the look of a possessed lunatic in his beady eyes.

"All what stuff? I didn't write anything. That was you!" Brittany snapped, trying to mask her nervousness with a healthy dose of attitude. Her arm was still keeping him at bay, while she searched for the door lever.

Suddenly, he dived toward her, clawing at her chest.

His fists felt like balls of iron hammering into her. Her shirt buttons went flying inside the dark car.

"What are you doing? Stop!" Brittany screamed.

He tugged at her jeans. She gripped her hands around his to stop him. He drew his hand back into a tight fist and struck the side of her face. Horrified, she put her hand to her face. She had never been hit before. Never had a fight, not even with her brother. But she had to do something. With her pulse slamming in her ears, Brittany swung her hand hard against his head knocking his cap into the back seat. Dante didn't stop. His eyes were fierce as he pulled at the clasp of her jeans. When he reached for the glove compartment, she began kicking wildly, like she, too, was possessed. Possessed with saving herself. Her life was in jeopardy. Her fingers scrambled around searching for the car door handle. She pulled but the door would not open. The glove compartment door fell open. She kicked ferociously and screamed while she felt around for the unlock button. She heard the sound of the automatic doors unlocking. Her hand searched again for the lever just as he withdrew his hand from the glove compartment. Screaming, she fell out of the car onto the ground. Dante gunned his engine and pulled away. "Wait, my purse!" Brittany yelled.

Within minutes, several people gathered around to help her. Adults came from surrounding houses. She didn't know how long she had been on the ground before she recognized Natasha, Shaniqua and Fabrianna pushing through the crowd. "Ohmigod Brittany, are you okay?" Natasha said.

Brittany's eyes were wide with fear and sadness. She

was trying her best to hold onto a shred of dignity. She would not cry, she couldn't cry. What had just happened to her, she wasn't even sure. She dusted her clothes off in a customary embarrassing fashion. She didn't even realize her shirt had been ripped open until Fabrianna placed a jacket over her.

"What happened?" Shaniqua said.

Tears surfaced in Brittany's eyes as she looked helplessly at her friends. Then she began crying. "I don't know. He just started attacking me, clawing at me like a madman."

Suddenly, a couple of Dekalb County patrol cars pulled up and two cops jumped out and ran over to Brittany. "Someone want to tell me what happened?" one of the officers said with a pad and pen in his hand.

With Natasha's arms draped across her shoulders, Brittany stepped forward and began explaining the incident as best she could between sniffles.

"How do you know the perpetrator?"

"We met on the Internet."

The police officer shook his head. "You need to come with us."

"Brittany, are you going to be okay?" Natasha asked. "Do you want me to come with you?"

"I'll be okay. Go ahead and take them home."

Natasha, Shaniqua and Fabrianna took turns hugging Brittany goodbye and offering words of encouragement.

During the ride home, Natasha and Shaniqua were discussing what they would have done while Fabrianna sat quietly in the back seat, staring vacantly out the window like she couldn't hear anything or anyone. When they reached Shaniqua's house, everyone said their goodnights. Fabrianna was on her way to her car when Shaniqua stopped her. "Girl, what's up with you, why are you so quiet?"

Fabrianna balled her small hand into a hard fist. The look in her eyes read kill and destroy by any means necessary. Shaniqua stepped back. "What did I do?"

A tear trickled down her friend's face. "Man, I hate that shit! That dude better be lucky I wasn't in my ride. That fool would have gotten blasted! That's why I don't like to ride in the car with other people."

Shaniqua wasn't sure how to respond. Fabrianna was violently upset. Her hands were still clenched into fists. She didn't know if she should try to talk to her or let her go. She didn't know if Fabrianna would hit her or what. "Well, you want to talk?"

"Naw, man, there's nothing to talk about. I want to hurt that fool," Fabrianna said, pacing down the sidewalk. A tear trickled down her face. She tried to wipe it quickly but Shaniqua had already seen it.

Shaniqua looked around to see if the nosey neighbors had heard anything. Everyone was always spying on each other like the CIA. If America really wanted to stop the war on terrorism, all they had to do was hire her grandmother and a few other senior citizens from the neighborhood. "You want to sit in your car for a minute?" She followed Fabrianna to the car. An uneasy silence lingered in the air along with the loud smelling coconut air freshener. Suddenly, Fabrianna pounded her fist against the dashboard. Shaniqua's head whipped around, her micros trailed. "Girl, are you okay?"

"Yeah, man, I just don't like that shit! He had no right!" she yelled, while her fist slammed against the dashboard again. Tears gushed out.

Shaniqua wasn't sure what to do. She couldn't understand why Fabrianna was reacting so strongly. It wasn't like she had been friends with Brittany. She watched Fabrianna begin to rock back and forth in the seat.

"He had no right! I hate him, I hate him!"

Shaniqua reached over to console her friend and to hold her tightly while she cried. She wanted desperately to ask what had happened. But deep down, she already knew.

Chapter 11

When the police car pulled into the Brown's large U-shaped driveway, bright chandelier lights were on as usual, signifying a member of the family was not home. Brittany hoped it was her dad who hadn't made it home yet. It would be much easier and less embarrassing to share the news with her mother. Her mother had a way of making the most embarrassing situations bearable, and sometimes even comical, she thought. At Brittany's twelfth birthday party, the DJ had all of her classmates from St. Joan Antida's middle school crammed onto the dance floor. Brittany remembered leaving her friends there sweating profusely while she ducked into the powder room to freshen up when suddenly she discovered drops of blood in her underwear. Fear and anxiety rushed her. She yelled through the bathroom door for at least twenty minutes until one of the kitchen helpers retrieved her mother. When Mrs. Brown finally arrived, tears had stained her daughter's face. Her mother immediately cradled her in her arms and planted tender kisses on her forehead. Brittany could still recall the soft and gentleness of her mother's voice when she spoke. "Everything's okay, sugarplum. There's nothing to be embarrassed about. As we discussed previously, this is your transition into womanhood. Now, don't get any grand ideas about being grown, because you're still my baby and will probably be even when you're nifty fifty!"

Nervous energy coursed through Brittany as the police officers escorted her to the door. What would her parents think when they saw the police standing beside her? Her face bruised, blouse torn. She rang the doorbell. Moments later, her dad opened the door slowly and methodically. Her heart sank deeper. He looked perplexed. Brittany's feet failed to carry her in. He slowly removed his cigar from the clutches of his lips and motioned for her to come inside. "Brittany, where's your key?"

"Evening, sir," one of the cops said.

"What's the meaning of this?" Mr. Brown said, looking back and forth between the cops and his daughter.

"It appears that your daughter was attacked this evening."

"Attacked? What! By who?"

Brittany's mother scurried down the long winding staircase. "What on earth?" She gently touched her daughter's chin and discovered the large bruise on her face. "Oh my God, are you alright?" her mother said, pulling her into her bosom. Brittany nodded and kept her focus on the swirls in the marble flooring. She really wanted to bury her face in her mother's chest. Crawl back inside the womb where it was safe. Mrs. Brown gently pushed her daughter back so that she could inspect her. "Where were you? What happened?"

Her father faced the officers. "What happened?" His tone was sharp, like the look in his eyes.

"Your daughter was allegedly attacked by someone at a party tonight."

Mr. Brown's nostrils flared. "Who is this someone?"

Brittany looked to the police officers to see if they would offer the information, but they remained silent. "His name's Dante Jenkins."

Mrs. Brown frowned. "Dante Jenkins? I never heard you mention him before."

"I met him on the Internet about six weeks ago?"

"The Internet?" Mr. Brown's voice was harsh and loud. "What? Have you lost your mind?"

"Albert," her mom offered.

The police officer interjected. "His name is allegedly Dante Jenkins. That's the name he gave to your daughter, sir."

her mother exclaimed, "Why in heavens did he attack you?"

Brittany continued to study the marble swirls on the floor. She could relate to the beige circular designs. That's how her life was, just a mass of swirls, no direction, no way out, just a whirl of confusion. A series of sniffles preceded her words. "I think he was trying to rape me."

Mrs. Brown wrapped her arms around her daughter again, squeezing tightly. "Oh no!" she gasped. "Oh dear, did he hurt you?"

The police officer interrupted. "Ma'am, your daughter was very fortunate and very smart. Luckily, she did not leave the premises with this guy. She fought him off and escaped from his car before he could drive off with her."

Mr. Brown looked at his daughter. "What were you doing in his car? Didn't Natasha pick you up?"

"Yes, but he met me at the party, so I felt obligated to talk to him. We sat down in his car for a little while."

The officer said, "Sir, Ma'am, what we would like to do is get another officer over here to analyze your computer to see if we can track this guy down. They'll probably have to take the computer to the precinct. If that's okay with you?"

"Yes, you have our full cooperation," Mr. Brown said, observing his wife and daughter.

"Sir, before we leave," the officer said, stopping in front of doorway. "I want to caution you to put on all safety locks and take extra precaution tonight."

Brittany saw her father's puzzled look. "He pulled off with my purse in his car."

"Oh, for heaven sakes!" her mother cried. "Can you please put an officer on night duty?"

"Ma'am, we'll try, but it's no guarantee."

After disclosing all the terrible details to her parents, Brittany's head felt like it was splitting in two. A penetrating migraine had positioned its claws around the left side of her head. Her stomach felt the hopelessness of being on a sinking ship, with no chance of survival. She lay in the bed, tossing and turning, but sleep would not come. With her eyes closed, Brittany tried to think of something positive to keep her mind off Dante. The more she tried not to think of him, the more she focused on him. His intense dark, beady eyes. His yellow-stained teeth. His odor. She slid out of bed and went over to the window. She peeked out the corner at the very bottom in case he was watching from behind a tree. She wondered if he would try to intrude her parent's home. The yard appeared as usual, nothing seemed to be moving. The night air was still and humid. Ducking from all the windows, Brittany made her way to the opposite end of the hallway where the alarm key pad was posted outside her parent's bedroom door. She had to make sure her dad had indeed secured the house.

Feeling a little more secure, she climbed back into bed and fell into a deep slumber. Before long, she was riding in the car. An unfamiliar car. Speeding. She was screaming at the driver to slow down. The driver kept going. Speeding. She looked around, but she didn't recognize her surroundings. She tried to unlock the car door. It refused to open. She yelled "Stop!" The driver kept driving. Speeding. She reached over to grab the steering wheel. The driver was a boy, but she couldn't make out his face. He wouldn't talk, his lips were clenched together. He just kept driving into the black night. Speeding. Brittany clawed at his arm to get him to stop. He faced her with a wide, scary grin. His teeth were yellow-green, resembling glow-in-the-dark vampire teeth.

His face remained non-descript, but his teeth were blinding her. She inched closer, starring at the driver, looking into his eyes. They were the saddest pair of eyes she had ever seen. They were so familiar. She had seen his eyes somewhere before. The driver began to cackle. His voice was scary. She leaned in closer to him. The long, well-defined bridge of his nose, the slight curl of bottom lip was that of Jared Hill. An earsplitting squeal erupted, jolting her from her sleep. She raised up to see the dawning of a new day through the window blinds. Sweat beads covered her back causing her lavender nightgown to cling to her skin. Breathless, with tears cascading down her face, Brittany looked at the clock; it was still too early to begin her day, but she was too afraid to go back to sleep.

Somewhere between dawn and the eight o'clock hour, sleep found her once more when suddenly a loud beeping sound from the home security alarm jolted her from awake. Someone had come through one of the five doors in the house. Her mind zipped to Dante. With lightening speed, she ran down the hallway to the security pad. She drew in a deep breath and held it so that she could listen to see if he was in the house. She heard nothing. Suddenly, the sound of footsteps came from the kitchen.

It had to be him. Hysteria coursed through Brittany, prompting her to barge into her parent's bedroom. "Dad, Mom, someone's in the house!"

Mrs. Brown shook her husband. "Honey, someone's downstairs!"

Her dad's snores immediately ceased. In one swift motion, he sprung into action; grabbed his handgun from the bottom nightstand drawer and made his way downstairs. Brittany and her mom watched from the upstairs landing, while Mr. Brown cocked his gun just outside the kitchen. "Who's there?"

"Yo, it's me, pops."

"Boy, you better let someone know the next time you come in here. What are you doing here so early?"

Brittany and Mrs. Brown came into the kitchen. "Yeah, Kevin, you scared us half to death." Brittany added, with one hand over her heart.

Kevin's gaze went from his dad to his mother and rested on Brittany. "Why are you all making a big deal? You know I come over sometimes and eat after I've been out. What's the deal?"

Mr. Brown took a seat at the kitchen table. "Your sister had an altercation last night with a boy."

Kevin put his sandwich down and stood up. "What boy?" He was tall and slender like his mother.

"No need to get worked up. The police on are on the case. But your sister left her purse in his car. So we're trying to be extra careful until we can get the locks changed."

Mrs. Brown started the coffee marker. "The locksmith will be here this morning."

The Brown family had an early breakfast together. Aside from going to Sunday Mass, Brittany stayed in the house the rest of the weekend. She didn't feel up to doing anything, especially not with that crazy man possibly still lurking around. She wanted to tell her parents about her recurring nightmares. She wanted to tell someone that Jared kept reappearing. Her parents had told her two years ago that she should have sought some type of counseling, some professional help to assist her in coping with his death, but she had always adamantly refused. Now, the nightmares were coming back again to haunt her. Jared's eyes were red, charred like coal, his voice cackling and piercing. It was getting out of control. She needed to talk to someone.

Chapter 12

A dark, purplish colored bruise sat on Brittany's face as she moved hastily through the school hallways Monday morning. There was no way to camouflage it, she had tried everything from her mother's make-up to Band-aids—nothing worked. On her way to her locker, a girl she vaguely recognized came up to her. "I heard what happened to you Friday night. Are you okay?"

Brittany offered a phony grin. "Of course."

Suddenly, an unidentified male voice shouted, "She ain't nothing but a tease! That's why she got what she deserved!"

"They're stupid. Don't listen to those guys. See you around," the girl said.

Brittany quickly scanned the hallway to see who had said it, but it was too crowded with a sea of faces staring right back at her. She rolled her eyes at whoever was staring and busied herself by digging around in her locker, hiding her humiliation.

Natasha and Shaniqua appeared. "Hey, Brittany," Natasha said, "How are you?"

"Never better," she said with a phony smile. "Other than this bruise on my cheek, he really didn't hurt me. I'm fine, girl please." She couldn't tell them that he had snatched her heart out of her chest. Not because she had loved him. She had never been in love with anyone. But because he had humiliated her in front of the whole school in the very last few weeks of school. She didn't want that to be how people remembered her. All the good she did to preserve her reputation had been sucked away in one swift draw, like a vacuum combing over a filthy carpet.

"Good, you sound like the same ol' Brittany." Shaniqua inched closer to her friend, "Brit, I'm not one to gossip, but you know the whole school's talking about Friday night."

Brittany's eyes darted back and forth between her friends. "So, I didn't do anything wrong," she retorted.

"Word is you led that boy on. That's why he was trying to rape you."

"I did not!" Her eyes were beginning to tear up. She had to blink them back down. Just because she had been victimized, she was not going to be the victim. Somewhere deep inside her, the anger began funneling its way to the forefront. "He was wrong for what he did. Not me! I did nothing wrong!"

Natasha draped her arm around Brittany's shoulders. "I know that and you know that, so you just have to ignore them."

"See, it doesn't feel too good to have people saying things about you that ain't true, does it?" Shaniqua said.

Brittany fired right back. "Shaniqua, the things they

were saying about you were true."

"Puh-lease," she said, planting her hands on her little hips. "Anywho! Moving right along. So what did you guys think of my girl, Fabrianna?"

Brittany smirked. "You mean your guy, Fabien?"

Shaniqua scrunched her face.

"That girl is gay as all get out!" Brittany said. "Looks like someone's been trying to reel her from a pond with that fish hook in her mouth."

"She's not gay!" Shaniqua snapped.

Brittany rolled her eyes toward Natasha who was busy scanning the area for Stephen. "Tell her, Tasha."

"Who am I to pass judgment?"

Brittany turned up the corners of her mouth. "Who said anything about passing judgment? It is what it is. My mother says, 'If it quacks likes a duck and walks like a duck, it must be a duck!' Your girl is gay as a jaybird. And she has the hots for you."

"No she don't!" Shaniqua bristled. "You need to worry about your own issues and get out of my business."

"What issues? I don't have any issues."

"Oh really," Shaniqua chuckled. "Oh, okay."

The school bell summoned the beginning of classes.

With her nose pointed toward the ceiling and squared

shoulders, Brittany strolled to class. She had done nothing wrong. Dante had no right to force himself on her. So what if she was sitting in his car, that didn't obligate her to become his little playmate, she thought as she retreated to the sanctity of her trigonometry class. For once, she was relieved not to have the cool, hip kids in her classes. She could easily escape the hushed whispers that hovered in the air all around her in the hallways.

When the school day ended, Brittany gathered her belongings and waited in the usual spot for one of her parents to pick her up. She missed her car so much. Emptiness welled up deep inside. Everything was going wrong. Why couldn't her dad wait to start building his own clinic after she was grown and gone? She wondered how long it would take before all the kids noticed that she didn't have the car any longer. They had already teased her last year because she thought she was getting a Lexus and ended up with a Honda. Now, she didn't even have the fricken Honda, she thought. Her parents were cruel. Evil.

Brittany saw Shaniqua's head poking out of the bus window and quickly turned her head in the opposite direction. "Brittany, where's your car?" Shaniqua yelled.

Brittany's eyes grew wide with embarrassment. Shaniqua had the loudest mouth she had ever heard. Some people would never have class no matter how much money they had, she thought. Like her mother always said, "The most ignorant people are always the loudest in the crowd." There was no way she was going to respond by yelling. *Simply uncouth.* Brittany offered a beauty queen wave goodbye, hoping no one in the surrounding area was paying close attention. Her thoughts shifted to Fabrianna. She felt bad about attacking Shaniqua's friend. Fabrianna had been there for her that terrible night by offering her a jacket. But for the moment, it felt good to put someone else in the hot seat, to take the focus off her. Brittany wondered if she was really becoming a social outcast.

A glistening, silver S500 pulled up in front of her. Her father should give up his ride, she thought as she made her way to the car. It was very strange for both parents to pick her up. Something was definitely up. Maybe they had just been playing a horrible, nasty joke on her and now, they were taking her to her car. Maybe it really did need to be serviced. Brittany offered a wide, toothy smile.

"Hey Mom, hey Dad."

Both parents responded with their usual inquisitive conversation. They were always fishing for clues about her school life. Her dad glanced at her through the rear-view mirror. "Have you seen any signs of that creep?"

"No, sir."

"Well, this is far from over. The police requested that we come to the precinct immediately. They would like to talk with us."

"Daddy, I don't want to go. I already told them everything that I know about him. I don't know anything else."

"Well, that's where we're going."

Minutes later, they were in the precinct. The two detectives assigned to the case escorted the Brown family into a small, bare room. "So, Brittany, how are you doing?" the much older detective asked.

She thought of telling them about the constant nightmares that she was having, but what could they do? They were hardly doing anything as it was. "Fine."

"Well, we have some information that we'd like to share with you," he said, pushing his glasses back onto the bridge of his nose. Brittany glared inquisitively at her parents, then turned her attention back to the detective. "Our computer forensics division has done a thorough analysis. And I'm afraid to tell you that the young man that you know as eighteen-year-old Dante, is actually twenty-six years old." Brittany gasped. Skimming through the file, the detective continued. "And his real name's Johnny Ashford. He resides in Columbia, South Carolina. He's wanted on several charges of committing lude acts with a minor and rape." The officer carefully removed his glasses, looked at Brittany's parents and then rested his eyes on Brittany. "I'm afraid this isn't the first time that he's done this sort of thing. He makes a game of posing as a younger guy to lure young girls into meeting him somewhere, then he assaults or rapes them."

"Oh, my," Brittany's mom said, shaking her head in disbelief. Brittany stared at the floor. There was nothing to say. What could she say?

"Brittany, you were very lucky," the second detective said, offering a reassuring nod. "We've been trying to catch this guy for a while. He's wanted in South Carolina, Alabama, and now, Georgia. Unfortunately, this sort of thing is happening more and more frequently."

Brittany's throat grew suddenly parched as if she had been stranded in the Sahara desert for days without water. No words surfaced. No tears threatened. She fidgeted with her fingers while a numbness overtook her as she reflected on the fact that she had entertained a serial rapist.

"Something has to be done to warn the kids of the dangers," Brittany's mom said. "My baby could have been murdered. My God!"

The younger detective nodded his agreement. "Ma'am, we travel around to the schools warning kids about the dangers, but they all seem to think that it can't happen to them." He turned toward Brittany. "Brittany, perhaps you could reach out to the other students to warn them. Maybe then kids would be more inclined to believe the danger is real and present."

Mrs. Brown beamed. "That's a wonderful idea."

Brittany eyes nearly popped out of her head. Had her mother completely lost her mind? There was no way she was about to put her personal business out there and let everyone snicker and crack jokes. *Oh, hell no! That's social suicide.* Things were already bad enough at school. "Sorry, I don't think that I would be right for that."

The good-natured detective smiled. "Well, if you change your mind, we'll be happy to use you. I think it would really help the kids to put a face with it. Kids are turning up missing every day at alarming rates."

With clenched jaws, Mr. Brown cleared his throat. "So, what exactly are you doing to catch this creep?"

"Sir, we're doing all that we can. We have a team of expert investigators on it right now. We'll let you know as soon as we have any new developments in the case. But in the meantime, we don't know his whereabouts, so stay alert."

Brittany left the precinct feeling no better than when she arrived. In fact, she felt worse. Stupid. How could she have been so naïve to believe "Dante"? He seemed like a real teenager. His MyPage looked authentic; Soulja Boy's music played, all of his friends were teens or music artists and his photos looked real. Brittany slumped in the backseat of the car, while her parents conversed. Her thoughts were miles away. She needed to escape, get out of Georgia. In college, none of this would matter.

Chapter 13

The halls were filled with noisy, meandering students as usual. It seemed the closer it got to the end of the school year, the less everyone seemed to care about tardiness. Natasha was causally scanning the hallway for Stephen. He had been avoiding her for the past couple of days. The ice was beginning to melt for her. She missed him. He had no right to be angry with her. She took her seat, ripped out a sheet of paper from her notebook and began writing.

> *Dear Stephen,*
>
> *I don't know what's bothering you, but we need to talk. I'm sorry if I hurt your feelings, but that was not my intention. Please meet me at my car, well my dad's car, after school if you want to talk.*
>
> *Hugs and kisses,*
>
> *Tasha*

She folded the note down to a paper football. When the bell rang, she made her way over to his locker and slid it between the cracks. She would have to wait all day to see how much he really valued their relationship.

Before she entered gym class, she had already told

herself, she was going to stay as far away from Adonis as possible. He was becoming increasingly difficult to ignore—tugging playfully at her hair or sitting so close he'd force her to move just to have room. The gym was packed with the normal chatter. Natasha stood next to the small bleachers waiting for the gym teacher when all of a sudden she felt warm, strong arms wrap around her. Silky black hairs were showcased on dark forearms. She spun around and smiled at Adonis. "Boy, what are you doing?"

"Oh, I can't hug you?" His soft smile and intense dark eyes were so inviting.

His infectious smile made Natasha smile. "Adonis, I already have someone."

"What does that have to do with me? I don't want him."

Coach Gilmore called PE class to order. Natasha quickly snapped out of the trance where Adonis' eyes held her captive. Maybe she didn't need a boyfriend, she thought.

After school, Natasha busied herself by digging around in the trunk of her dad's car. Nate had left smelly socks, empty water and Gatorade bottles. He could have at least had the decency to clean it out when he left for college, she thought. She made a mental note to get him to clean it out the next time he came home. The University of Georgia wasn't that far away, and he often caught a ride home with another member from the basketball team. As soon as Natasha slammed the trunk closed, she saw Stephen approaching. His pink, plump lips looked as pouty as a three-year-old kid who had just been told that he couldn't have ice cream until after dinner. She grinned to help ease the awkwardness. "Hey, Stephen."

"What up?"

Natasha thought his response was distant, especially after not seeing each other in days. Usually, he greeted her with a hug. They agreed last year that they were not going to be the type of couple who "bust slob" in the hallways, making other kids yell, "Get a room!" But he could have at least responded a little warmer than that. Maybe he was really ready to end the relationship and rather than tell her, he was going to start acting like a jerk. That way she would have the hard job of ending the relationship. Her mom always said that women were better at breaking up than men were. In fact, her mom hadn't ever recalled a guy breaking up with her in all her years of dating. When Natasha's eyes met Stephen's, she offered him a sympathetic smile. "What's wrong with you?"

"Nothing." Stephen hung his hands in his pockets fiddling around with something. His expression was the most serious one she had ever seen him wear. He had always been very easy going.

"Well," Natasha said.

"Well, what?"

Now, Natasha knew with certainty they were over. It had been a good eighteen months, she thought. Most relationships didn't last longer than a month in high school. "Well, I don't know what to say," Natasha said, her eyes tearing up a little. She hoped nobody was watching. All the yellow school buses had already driven away.

"Let me make this easy for you. Here, take this," Stephen said, pulling out a gold, heart shaped ring with a sparkling ruby mounted inside. "I was going to give it to you last Friday at dinner."

Natasha's mouth was wide open as if someone had anchored her bottom lip. "Ah! I don't know what to say."

"You don't have to say anything. Just take it as a reminder of me. I've had it for some time now and I was waiting for the right time to give it to you. In the meantime, I lost the receipt," Stephen said with a nervous laugh. "So I still want you to have it. Maybe you can remember me from time to time if you aren't too busy."

Natasha studied Stephen. She now knew with certainty what the whole issue was about. "Stephen, it's not that I'm too busy. I just—"

"Tasha, you're busy making all these plans for the future and none of them include me. You want to go off to Paris, but I thought we were going to go to college together."

She moved closer to him. "Stephen, I'm sorry if you feel like I don't value our relationship, but I do. And also, I haven't decided what I'm doing after graduation. I'm still thinking it through. But that doesn't mean that I don't want you in my life now."

"Graduation's a month away."

"I know, Stephen, just give me some time. Let's not end it this way." Natasha stretched her arms toward Stephen. Slowly, he offered a half-hearted hug.

He shrugged under the hot sun. Beads of perspiration curled the hair around his hairline. "Alright, well, my dad's expecting me at the shop. I have to go." And without warning, Stephen stalked away.

Annoyed, Natasha watched him. Everyone had been saying that he was going to start pressuring her, but she had no idea it would be for a lifelong commitment. Well, at least it felt like that. In some ways, she wished that he was putting the pressure on her to have sex, because she had already been prepared to handle that one. She was going to tell him that she still wasn't ready and if he felt the need to go down that road, then he was free to go with someone else. She was going to hold true to the morals and values that her parents instilled in her. But this was different. She didn't have a rebuttal for this type of pressure.

Chapter 14

After school, Shaniqua went home instead of going directly to work as she did most days. When she entered the townhouse, the smell of simmering collard greens welcomed her. Plump sweet potatoes decorated the shabby kitchen table that should have been discarded years ago. Suddenly, She threw her backpack down and scurried over to her grandmother, who was slumped at the table, raking the knife slowly over a yam. "Granny, are you alright?"

"I got a shootin' pain in my arm and chest," she said, with the knife barely grazing the potato skin. "I guess I'm just a lil tired. That's all, baby. How you?"

"Granny, go upstairs and rest. I'll finish."

Using the bottom of her apron, her grandmother dried her hands. "Don't you have to be to work?"

"Yes, ma'am, but, I'll call in. I've never called in before so they'll understand."

"I don't want you messin' up your job, baby. A good job's hard to come by these days. I been taking care of myself for a long time. I'll be alright. And what I can't do, the good Lawd'll see me through. Ya hear?"

"Yes, ma'am," she said, reaching for the phone. She dialed the number to the store, and when the assistant manager answered, she wanted to hang up. But she knew her grandmother needed her more. "Ursula, my grandmother's sick, I can't make it today."

"Shaniqua, you're supposed to close the store tonight. If we can't depend on you, then we'll have to find someone else."

"Is Cindy there?"

"Nope, and she's going to tell you the same thing."

"Ursula, my grandmother is sick," Shaniqua pleaded.

"Oh, well."

Anger churned deep within her and forced a tear to surface. Shaniqua couldn't believe anyone could be so coldhearted. She had been an excellent employee for the last year—perfect attendance, the cash register always balanced, friendly to customers, even the ones she didn't like. She drew in her bottom lip and sucked on it, trying to decide what to do. After a few seconds of silence, she spoke. "Do what you have to do!" Then she slammed the phone down like she was slamming it against Ursula's head.

Her grandmother had overheard the phone conversation. "Chile, I told you I be just fine. You go on and go to work, here. Never you mind me."

"No! Your health is more important than some stupid job, Granny. They can fire me for all I care!" she said, helping her grandmother out of the chair. She didn't really know how old her grandmother was, because every time she asked, Granny would say, "Stay in a chile's place." She escorted her upstairs and tucked her in the bed the way her grandmother had done her so many nights when she was little or sick. "Alright, Granny, when dinner's ready, I'll bring your plate."

"No, baby. I'll come down. You know I don't allow no eatin' in the bedrooms."

She quietly closed Granny's bedroom door. To argue was useless. Her grandmother had to be the most strong-willed, stubborn person she knew. Her thoughts floated back to Ursula as she proceeded downstairs to the kitchen. From the moment they met a few weeks ago, Shaniqua could tell that Ursula Moore was going to be trouble. Shaniqua had changed one of the mannequin's outfits without being asked to as she occasionally did when she was bored and there weren't any customers. Suddenly, Ursula came charging into the backroom, "Who changed the damn mannequin?"

"Shaniqua," Cindy, the manager who originally hired Shaniqua, said, "It looks great, doesn't it?"

"She changed some thangs she had no business changin'," Ursula said, speaking loudly enough for Shaniqua to overhear.

Shaniqua knew had they been in elementary school, she would have politely escorted Ursula out to the playground and beat the crap out of her to shut her big mouth. Because Ursula was conspicuously nosey, it hadn't taken long for coworkers to assign her the nickname, "Snoop Doggy Dog." Ursula was short which made her look younger than her real age, thirty-nine. Layers of orange-blond weave engulfed her tiny head, while devilish-looking eye contacts popped out of her face. If ever there was a woman to prove that not all Georgia women were peaches, then Ursula was it. In fact, Shaniqua thought she'd be better characterized as an "alley cat" from Atlanta.

Shaniqua pulled the pot roast out of the oven and stuck two plump sweet potatoes pies inside. Granny always made an extra pie for someone at church. Shaniqua had no clue who the other pie was for this time. She sliced through the tender meat and piled it on her grandmother's plate along with a helping of rosemary potatoes, carrots and collard greens.

She listened for movement upstairs. There was none. The floor boards weren't creaking from the weight of her grandmother. The television wasn't on; only the constant hum from the window air condition could be heard. Her grandmother was finally getting some much-needed rest. Shaniqua tiptoed upstairs and gently pushed her bedroom door open. The creaking door usually alerted her grandmother. Granny had always been a very light sleeper. But this time she didn't move. Shaniqua inched closer to see her grandmother was sprawled across the bed, her hands clutching her chest. The plate crashed to the floor. Tiny pieces of china, her grandmother's good plate, scattered across the wooden floor, the juice from the pot roast and greens splattered the walls. She rushed to her grandmother's side. Granny's mouth was open; her face was scrunched in pain. Shaniqua clawed at the phone, her fingers trembling as she dialed 9-1-1. The operator answered, "DeKalb County Operator 15, what's your emergency?"

"Help me! My grandmother's sick!"

"Calm down. I need some information from you."

Shaniqua burst into tears. "We need some help now!"

"What's wrong with your grandmother?"

"I don't know. She's lying in the bed with her mouth wide open."

"Is she still breathing?"

"I think so. I don't know. Please hurry. Hurry!" She gave the operator the address and then phoned her cousin Nee Nee. No one answered, so she left a frantic message. She kneeled down beside her grandmother. She felt so helpless. She wished that she could give her mouth-to-mouth resuscitation, but she never paid attention in health class when they were teaching it. She touched Granny's cheek, she still felt warm. Shaniqua ran down the stairs, taking several at a time, and waited for the ambulance. They were taking too long. She ran back upstairs. She put her cheek next to her grandmother. "Granny, don't leave me. Please don't leave me. I need you. Please Granny," she pleaded, rocking back and forth with her grandmother in her arms. "God, please don't take Granny away from me."

Suddenly a voice boomed, "Step away!"

Shaniqua looked up; it was the paramedics pushing through the bedroom door with a stretcher. She jumped back and the emergency workers sprang into action. One worker pulled out a heart defibrillator. The other ripped Granny's housedress in half. "Ma'am, can you please step out of the room?"

Shaniqua moved into the hallway and watched while they worked on her grandmother. Her mind was swirling around. How could God want to take her grandmother away from her? What did she do to deserve this? Granny had always been good—good to everyone who knew her. She even gave food from her own kitchen to the homeless people around the corner. Shaniqua wondered if she should call her aunt Kathy, the only other somewhat responsible family member. Her mother was nowhere to be found. Her uncles were probably somewhere drunk.

The paramedics wheeled her grandmother out on the stretcher.

"Where are you taking her?" Shaniqua shouted.

"Grady, get the door," the man shouted to the other worker.

Shaniqua hurried back inside and telephoned Granny's good friend, Dorothy Mae. "Ms. Dorothy Mae, this is Bessie Williams' granddaughter, Shaniqua. Something's wrong with Granny. They're taking her down to Grady Hospital."

"Why are they taking her all the way down there instead of DeKalb Memorial?"

"I don't know. Can you please come get me and take me down there?"

"Of course, doll, I be right over."

Shaniqua hung up the phone. Her nerves were raw. She didn't know what she would do if something happened to her grandmother. She was her entire world. She loved Granny more than she loved anything or anyone. God had no right to take her grandmother, the only person who had ever loved her.

When Shaniqua arrived at the hospital, she bolted out of car and hurried into the emergency room. She needed to be away from her grandmother's friend, even if only for a couple of minutes. All that talk about how God was good and how He didn't make mistakes was only making her feel worse, not better. The emergency room was full. There was a long line of people waiting at the information desk. Dorothy Mae wobbled in on her cane a few minutes later. Shaniqua felt bad that she wasn't able to wait on her grandmother's friend, but this was no time for good manners. Granny would just have to understand. Her life was on the line. Shaniqua tapped her foot, waiting for some woman to finish asking a stupid question about the cafeteria's location. Who the heck cares? There were three people in front of her. Shaniqua paced back and forth. Finally, it was her turn. "Hello, my name's Shaniqua Williams. They just brought my grandmother, Bessie Williams, in the ambulance a little while ago."

The receptionist keyed some information into the computer and then looked over some papers sitting on the desk. "I'm sorry. No Bessie Williams has been checked in."

"Ma'am, she has to be here. I saw them take her away."

The receptionist quickly responded, "I'm sorry, I don't know what else to tell you."

Tears welled up in Shaniqua's eyes. Her voice broke into a soft cadence, "She has to be here." She took off toward the huge oversize double doors and pulled on them, but they would not open! The person that had the power to unlock the doors was staring at her with angry eyes. "Young lady, if you don't move away from the doors, I'll have no choice but to call security."

Dorothy Mae walked over and draped her arm around Shaniqua's shoulders and said to the receptionist, "We're sorry, Miss. We believe her grandmother just had a heart attack. So now tell me, is there another hospital they could have taken her to?"

"Where was she when the ambulance picked her up?"

"At home?"

"What county, ma'am?"

"Oh, yes, yes, I'm sorry. DeKalb County, Lithonia."

"Ma'am, more than likely, they would have taken her to the hospital there. DeKalb Memorial."

"The man told me Grady," Shaniqua cried out.

The receptionist ignored Shaniqua and kept her attention on Dorothy Mae. "Here's their phone number if you would like to call."

Shaniqua dialed the number on her cell. "I'm looking for a patient by the name of Bessie Williams."

"Who's calling please?" the receptionist said.

"This is her granddaughter."

There was silence for a moment. Shaniqua could hear the typing of computer keys. "She's recovering in room 326. I can connect you to the nurse's station if you like."

"Yes, please." Shaniqua nodded so that Dorothy Mae and the receptionist would know that her grandmother was there.

Moments later, another person was on the line. "Hello?"

"This is Bessie Williams' granddaughter. How's she doing?" Shaniqua held her breath while she waited for the response.

"She suffered a heart attack. However, she's in stable condition, but I would urge you to come as quickly as you can."

Tears filled Shaniqua's eyes once more. "We're on our way."

Dorothy Mae drove ten miles under the speed limit the entire way to the hospital. Shaniqua wished she knew how to drive. When they finally reached DeKalb Memorial, she made her way quickly to her grandmother's room while Dorothy Mae parked her car in the parking garage. When Shaniqua walked into the hospital room, she saw Granny's lifeless frame lying in the bed with an IV cabled through her. An oxygen mask covered half her face. Shaniqua was so nervous, she thought she was going to vomit on the freshly waxed floor. Her grandmother's eyelids were closed with finality like they would never open again. Shaniqua took Granny's hand and stroked the back of her soft, wrinkled skin. These hands had been so good to her, bathing her, cooking and sewing for her. They held her firmly in love and discipline so many times, creating crooked ponytails and leg-stinging switches. Granny's large frame was soft and still as the nurse put a hypodermic needle into her arm. Shaniqua winced. She didn't like needles, blood, or anything to do with hospitals. She managed to stomach it when Brittany was in the hospital two years ago. Shaniqua could count the number of times she had visited Brittany on one hand. She hated hospitals, but she would stay here a lifetime if it would heal Granny, she thought, as the nurse put a clean bandage on her grandmother's hand. "Is my grandmother going to be okay?"

"She suffered a stroke," the nurse said gently as Dorothy Mae entered the hospital room.

"A stroke? Someone told me a heart attack. Which is it?"

The nurse looked at her grandmother's chart. "You're right. I'm so sorry."

Shaniqua grimaced. She had heard about hospital workers being careless and misdiagnosing people. Under no circumstances was she going to leave her grandmother's side so they could treat her for the wrong ailment. The nurse offered an apologetic smile. "We'll watch over her the next couple of days."

Shaniqua rolled her eyes. She had no faith in the nurse. She thought of requesting someone else. Shaniqua rested her cheek against the top of her grandmother's head. So many tubes were attached to her body. She couldn't lose Granny. "Is there anything I can do?"

"Right now, we'll just have to wait to see what kind of damage was done. Is this her sister?" the nurse said, looking at Dorothy Mae.

Dorothy Mae shook her head. "I'm just a good friend. Me and Bessie been friends a long time."

"Well, I need an adult next of kin? Is someone here?"

"No, ma'am," Shaniqua said. "I can call my aunt Kathy."

"And I already called Pastor Cosby," Dorothy Mae said. "He's on his way."

Shaniqua quickly telephoned the rest of Granny's family. Everyone except her own mother. No one knew where she was or how to contact Karen. Her feelings would never change for her mother.

A couple of hours later, the waiting room was so full of family and church members that the hospital requested that some of the visitors leave. Shaniqua didn't care who chose to leave, she was going to be by her grandmother's side all night even though her condition had now been upgraded to stable.

The next morning, the nurse came in to check on Granny and explained that the doctors would be running a series of tests to see if the heart attack had caused any permanent damage. They wheeled Granny in and out for hours. Shaniqua was busy watching television when she heard a light tapping at the door. "Come in," she said.

The heavy wooden door swung open. A large bouquet of flowers were moving toward Shaniqua. A little head peaked around a lily. "Hey girl, I got your message. I thought I would surprise you."

A soft smile framed Shaniqua's tired face. "Fabrianna, you didn't have to do that."

"I know, but I wanted to. I'm really sorry about your grandmother."

She nodded. "Thanks."

"I didn't know if you had eaten, so I brought you something."

"Wow, that's so sweet of you," Shaniqua said, reaching out for a hug.

The two friends locked in a warm embrace. Shaniqua's mind raced back to Brittany's paranoia about Fabrianna being gay. Shaniqua had to dismiss that, Fabrianna was a good friend.

Chapter 15

Natasha was stretched out across her bed flipping through a fashion magazine, renewing her motivation and courage to face her parents. She was rehearsing her persuasive argument about modeling in Paris when she heard her father's car pull into the driveway. In just a few minutes, she thought, her parents would tell her just how proud of her and this opportunity they were. She wasn't a hundred percent sure of how her mother was going to respond, but she had a secret weapon that she planned to unleash. She closed her bedroom door behind her and made her way down to the family room. She glanced at the framed pictures on the wall. The whole wall was covered with photos of the entire family, smiling and happy. Life was so much simpler ten years ago, she thought. Even though her parents were divorced, she really couldn't complain. Her dad was still very active in parenting. The one thing she could complain about she couldn't do anything about—she looked just like him, except she was female. Extended family members always joked that her daddy had birthed her, not her mother. Her father was already in the den when she entered, "Hi, Princess," he said.

"Hi, Dad." She kissed him and took a seat on the sofa next to her mom.

"So, Princess, what's this I hear about you wanting to go to Paris to model instead of going to college?"

Natasha fiddled with her fingers. Her nerves were in her stomach. She looked at her mom, who sat stone-faced, her arms clamped tightly across her chest. Her mother was definitely ready to do battle. She was probably sitting on heavy artillery waiting to go in for the kill. She should have taken a seat next to her dad, Natasha thought as she swallowed hard. "Well, Dad, I've done my research and it's a very reputable agency. Monsieur Jean-Pierre Marais, the agent, said that I could live with other models-girls in an apartment and we'd split the rent four ways."

Her mother's eyebrows curled, creating a deep, angry furrow across her forehead. "And so what about Savannah State?"

"I still want to go to college. I just want to put it off for just a year to give modeling a shot."

"Absolutely not!" her mother said sternly. "You will go to college and get your degree! And then give modeling a try."

"Mom, Monsieur Marais said that I was going to make a lot of money and that I would be able to pay my own tuition for all four years when I do go to college."

Ms. Harris kept her smoldering eyes fixed on Natasha. "Well, as far as I'm concerned, I'm not discussing this any further with a child. You don't have enough sense to know what's best for you right now. I will not allow you to mess up your life. You're not going and that's final! Up to your room!"

Natasha turned to her dad with pleading eyes. He always seemed to understand her better than her mom did.

"Now!" her mother ordered.

Angrily, Natasha stalked up the stairs, nearly choking on the words held prisoner in her throat. She didn't even have the opportunity to pull her ace card. The plan was to try it the respectful way first and if that failed, she was going to tell them that she was turning eighteen years old twenty-three days after graduation and she no longer needed their permission to make her life decisions. With tears clouding her vision, she slammed her bedroom door shut and plopped down across her bed. This was her big opportunity to make something of herself and they weren't allowing her to take advantage of it. What was the point of spending all that money on modeling classes if they weren't going to let her model?

She whipped out her miniature photo album from her nightstand drawer and searched the photos until she found her favorite picture. At age five, Natasha was dressed in a pink ruffled dress, walking hand in hand with her mother during an Easter egg hunt at the church. She removed the picture and tore off a little piece of the photograph. Her mom was being ridiculous, she thought. Natasha had always been a good person, a good student, a good daughter. She was still going to attend college and become a Delta just like her mom. She ripped another piece of the photograph just above her mother's head. Bitterness and resentment clipped the corners of her mouth tight together, while tears streamed down her face. She never thought she would really say this and mean it, but she was beginning to detest her mother. She couldn't get away from her quick enough. She ripped her mother's head off and cried herself to sleep.

Chapter 16

After several nights of enduring restless sleep on the hard hospital cot, Shaniqua slept well in her own bed. It felt good to be home again; most important, she was grateful to have her grandmother home even though she was immobile. Her presence was enough to make her granddaughter smile again. Passing days and nights in the hospital not knowing if her grandmother would ever come home again had been tumultuous. She had missed several days of school and work, but her grandmother's health came first. As Pastor Cosby told Shaniqua, "The Angel of Death had knocked on the door, but God told him to go away, it wasn't her grandmother's time."

Shaniqua showered and dressed in a black miniskirt and an off the shoulder white top. Peeking into her grandmother's room, she saw the nurse, Ms. Cassandra, checking her grandmother's blood pressure. "Granny, I'm getting ready to leave for school now."

Her grandmother barely lifted her arm to wave goodbye. With anxiety coursing through her, Shaniqua motioned for the nurse to step outside of the room for a chat. "Ms. Cassandra, I won't be at school today because we have a field trip. So if you need anything, call me on my cell."

Ms. Cassandra lips parted into a soft smile making her plump cheeks appear even plumper, like a cuddly, teddy bear. "Where are you going on your field trip?"

Shaniqua searched the hallway for the answer, making a mental note to knock down the big cobweb in the corner. Time was ticking slowly. The dull eggshell-colored walls were screaming for a fresh coat of paint. She hated to lie at a time like this, but everyone had been talking about senior "skip out" day. She didn't want to be the only person who had missed out, besides Brittany and Natasha. They were squares, so they didn't count, she thought. Her mind raced back to her fourth grade field trip. "Oh, uh, we're going down to Martin Luther King's birthplace."

The nurse's face lit up. "It's so inspiring to be down there. You can just feel the presence of greatness all around Auburn Avenue and the King Center. There's so much to see. Have a great time."

Shaniqua left the house feeling bad, remembering the time when Granny had come along on the field trip to Dr. King's birthplace, beaming with pride as she went in and out of the different rooms where a great man had been born. A man who had done so much for his people and the world, all through nonviolence. Each time they left a room, Granny would whisper, "Oh, yeah, the Kings' had some money. Poor folks didn't live like this in my day." All the kids who were in earshot would snicker. Shaniqua stood on the corner in the warm morning sun, letting the rays refresh her, waiting for Fabrianna. Maybe they could at least ride past his birthplace, she thought.

Piedmont Park was packed as usual. Students from all areas of metropolitan Atlanta were there. It had been deemed the official senior skip out spot. A variety of groups sprawled over the park, some around the lake, others gathered on the ball fields. Fabrianna and her group found a large shade tree to call home for the day. When Shaniqua met her friends, it didn't take long for her to realize that the girls were coupled up. Brittany's voice boomed in her head, "Your girl is gay as a jaybird!" She and Fabrianna took a seat on the blanket next to a girl that looked so much like a boy, except the little hills of her breast had given it away.

As the girls relaxed under the shady tree, eating vegetable chips and drinking organic juice, as they discussed their future plans. Shaniqua listened quietly as they chatted about which colleges they would be attending. She was still uncertain about her future. Her grandmother's health was her first priority. All of a sudden, a mob of people began running their way. Shaniqua instinctively sprung to her feet. "What's going on?"

"Come on, everybody, let's go!" Fabrianna said. "Grab your stuff! Hurry!"

Shaniqua watched Fabrianna's friends scatter like

roaches. "What's going on?"

"Run!" Fabrianna shouted while sprinting off.

Shaniqua quickly scanned the area for terrorists, a dog, a gunfight, something. A mob of kids were running toward her. She lost sight of Fabrianna. Suddenly, at least fifty police officers appeared. Some with dogs. Some already had students handcuffed. Fight or flight energy ran through her and without warning, her feet carried her away so fast, she didn't even realize it. Her four-inch heel snapped in two. A mass of people sandwiched together slowed the crowd's movement. The police were gaining ground. Using her bony elbows and knobby knees, she pushed and nudged her way through. Her toes were being severely trampled on, but she couldn't feel the pain. Her mind was on not going to jail. It would kill her grandmother, she thought. Then she'd be just like the rest of the Williams's with police records. The cops were only a few feet away from her when they snatched up another girl. She would be next. She had to do something to escape. Suddenly, she broke off from the crowd, running so fast, she felt like she wasn't running at all, but gliding through the air like a bird. Fabrianna's car was her target. She saw her friend yelling out of the window, but her nerves wouldn't allow her to make sense of it. She charged across the street and made it to the car. Her fingers moist with sweat prevented her from opening the car door. Fabrianna leaned over and opened it for her. Shaniqua plopped down in the passenger seat. "Go!"

Plump pillows cradled Shaniqua as she stretched out across her bed and sifted through the day's events. She needed time to process it all. Had she really been that close to going to jail and getting a record? Her thoughts floated back to Jordan Kelley. Partly because of her, he had a record. She wondered where he was. No one had heard from him. She shook the guilt from her mind. She couldn't allow herself to feel bad about calling the cops on him. He was a drug dealer who was doing nothing more than bringing down his own people. The last thing the world needed was one more young black man poisoning the minds and bodies of more young black men and women. Her conscious was clear. She had done the right thing.

Her thoughts drifted again to the day's events. So much had happened. So many feelings to sort through. All day long, she had been confused by the manner in which Fabrianna's friends were responding to her. They kept saying things like, "Fabrianna, yo' girl ain't going to put up with your crazy behind for very long." And then all the girls would giggle and look back and forth between Shaniqua and Fabrianna. She wondered if they thought that she and Fabrianna were a couple as well. But by the end of the day, Fabrianna had removed all the uncertainty. Fabrianna had changed their relationship and Shaniqua wasn't sure what to do about it. Tired of thinking, she welcomed the opportunity to doze off. Suddenly, she was snapped back to reality with a light tapping at her bedroom door. "Yes?"

"I'm getting ready to leave in a few moments, as soon as I give your grandmother her last dose of medicine for the evening," Ms. Cassandra said.

Shaniqua trailed the nurse back into her grandmother's room and observed her as she administered the medication. Shaniqua was so grateful to this nurse for taking care of her grandmother. Ms. Cassandra did every thing with such patience and compassion, as if she was taking care of her own grandmother. She wondered if Ms. Cassandra always knew that she wanted to be a nurse. Everyone in the world seemed to know which direction he or she wanted to go in after graduation, except her. Brittany was going to college somewhere and at least Natasha knew she wanted to go to Paris to model even though her parents forbid it. Shaniqua hadn't even put in any applications to any college, not even the beauty college. She took a seat in the corner and watched the nurse work. "Ms. Cassandra, may I ask you something?"

The nurse looked up. "Sure, sugar, ask me anything."

"Did you always know you wanted to be a nurse?"

Ms. Cassandra put down the pill bottle. "No, not really. I never thought about it. Truthfully, I hated school."

Shaniqua grinned. "You?"

"Yes. I wanted to travel and see the world, so I joined the Navy. While I was there, I was trained to be a medical assistant. I did four years and after that, I got out. And I realized that I really liked helping people. So the military paid for me to go to school to get my nursing degree."

"So you didn't have to pay any money for college?"

"Nope, not a dime."

"Wow! That's great. So you really like taking care of people?"

"Yes, sugar. I get to meet a lot of nice people." The nurse smiled. "I see that you do a great job of taking care of your grandmother." Have you ever thought about going to school for nursing? Shaniqua shrugged. "I don't think I could do that for a complete stranger."

"Sure you could, sugar. All it takes is a caring spirit. The spirit to serve—to want to help people as best you can."

"Do they pay good?"

"Yes, it pays very well. And there's a shortage of nurses. You finish nursing school and you won't have a problem getting a job."

Shaniqua studied Ms. Cassandra's movement, while her mind roamed. She had never really considered going to college. If she did go, how would she pay for it? There was no way she could leave Granny for four years to go into the military. That was out of the question. She had to think of something else. Maybe she would talk with Mrs. Smith, the Guidance Counselor. Suddenly the phone rang, jarring her. "Hello?"

"Shaniqua, this is Ursula from work. You're late!."

"Late? How am I late when I wasn't scheduled to come in?"

"When you called and told Cindy that your grandmother

was out of the hospital, I left a message on your phone that I was putting you back on the work schedule immediately."

"Well, I didn't get the message."

"Well, that's your problem, now isn't."

Shaniqua had to bite her tongue to prevent from telling her what she really thought of her. *Fat, lazy lima bean!* "There's no one to see after my grandmother right now. The nurse leaves every day at 5:00 p.m."

"Well, I guess I'll just have to put you down as a no-show. One more and you'll be fired! Do we have an understanding?"

Tears welled in her eyes. Shaniqua never thought she could dislike a person as much as she disliked Ursula. She was an evil witch with a black heart. If Cindy, the manager, wasn't making a big fuss about her not being able to come to work, then why would the assistant manager? "Fine. Ursula, do what you have to do."

"I certainly will."

Shaniqua heard the line go dead. Granny was awake and looked at her with suspicious eyes. She tried not to talk much, because it took too much energy. "Go, go." Granny's voice was soft as a feather.

"No, Granny, I'll be fine." Shaniqua walked Ms. Cassandra to the door.

"I gave your grandmother her medication; she should be fine until I return in the morning. Just make sure she isn't getting too warm during the night."

"Okay."

"Think about the profession. Nurses make a lot of money and we're in high demand."

Shaniqua nodded and bid her goodnight. Her mind raced back to Ursula. She had to figure out a way to keep from losing her job. Yet, there was no way she could return. Her grandmother needed to be under constant supervision. What if Granny needed a drink of water? What if she needed to go to the bathroom? Who would help her? Her grandmother had stood by her when no one else had. And now all she had to do was look after Granny in the evenings. Ursula might as well fire her. No job, no money, no nothing would ever come between them.

Chapter 17

Monday morning, Brittany and Natasha were in the courtyard catching up on the weekend's events when Shaniqua appeared. "Hey, y'all!"

"So, how was senior skip out day on Friday?" Brittany said, offering a sour smile. "Did y'all get drunk like everyone else?"

"Girl, we were sipping organic juice and eating squirrel food until the police raided the park."

"What! See, that's why I didn't go," Brittany said. "I do not have time to get locked up for skipping school. It is not that serious for me."

Shaniqua wondered if she should tell her friends about her and Fabrianna. But she really hadn't decided how she felt about it. Fabrianna was a really nice person. But she had never thought of herself as a lesbian. She drew in a deep, calculated breath. If her friends were her friends, then they would be there for her no matter what she decided about her sexual preference. She smiled. "Brittany, you were right about Fabrianna."

Brittany smacked her hands together in a thunderous

clap. "See, Tasha, I told you! Girlfriend was just waiting for the right opportunity. Trust me, I know."

Shaniqua frowned. "Brittany, who made you an authority on every subject? Dang! Everything that happens either you have been there done that, or your mother has been there done that or somebody that Brittany Brown knows has been there done that!"

"It is what it is. Don't hate the player, hate the game. So, what did she do?"

Shaniqua took a moment to collect her thoughts and then a slight smile creased her mouth. "She didn't attack me like you're thinking."

"You sound as though you liked it?"

"I just think she's a nice person, that's all."

Brittany turned to Natasha. "You hear this crap?"

Natasha offered an indifferent nod. "So, are y'all going to start going out?"

Shaniqua shrugged.

"Girl, you have lost your ever-lovin' mind? Just because you had one bad experience with a boy does not mean you have to become a lesbian!"

"This has nothing to do with Jordan. I just think she's a nice person."

"There are plenty of nice people in the world. That doesn't mean that you have to go out with them."

"We're not going out. It was just a kiss. That's all!"

"What! Ohmigod! You kissed her?"

"For your information, I didn't kiss her. She kissed me."

Brittany sneered. "Right, big difference. I don't care who kissed who, that's just nasty."

"It wasn't a tongue kiss."

"Tasha, you need to help your friend, because she's seriously confused."

"I'm not!"

"Girl, your head is gone. Tell her, Tasha."

Both girls looked to Natasha, sandwiching her between their opposing beliefs. Sometimes she hated that they always made her the authority on everything. Her mother always taught her to be slow to speak, because once you put words out there, you can't take them back. Words could be lethal weapons. Natasha turned to Brittany first. "Girl, you have to be more accepting of people who don't necessarily share your beliefs."

Brittany rolled her eyes. "Puhlease."

"Seriously Brit, for instance, you're Catholic, right? Well, there are things that I don't agree with about your religion."

"Like what?" Brittany retorted.

"That's just my point. It doesn't matter. You have to be willing to live and let die," Natasha said, then turned to face Shaniqua. "Let me ask you something, have you always had feelings for girls?"

"No, of course not. I just think Fabrianna's very nice."

Brittany pursed her lips. "Like I said, 'there are a lot of nice people in the world. That don't mean you're gay." It's just a fad, if you ask me. Look at all these queers running around the daggone school." Brittany glanced at the lunchroom patrons. "So let me guess, y'all going to prom together as a couple now?"

"Maybe! Who are you going with? Dante!"

Both friends stared at Shaniqua like she was crazy.

They couldn't believe that she would say something so hurtful. Sudden tears surfaced in Brittany's eyes. She was just a blink away from them cascading down her face.

Just then Stephen came and sat down, ceasing the previous conversation. Shaniqua toyed with her food while Brittany excused herself from the lunch table. There was no way Shaniqua was about to go with Brittany. She didn't feel like listening to anything else she had to say. Shaniqua could tell that Stephen was waiting for her to leave, too. "Alright, y'all, I get the message!" Shaniqua said, packing up her belongings.

❧

Stephen took a seat next to Natasha. "Hey, what's up?"

"Nothing."

Stephen looked at Natasha's bare fingers. "So you're not wearing your ring?"

"Nope."

"Why not?"

"Because we're not like that. Stephen, I called you all weekend and you didn't return my calls. I'm just not feeling this unnecessary drama."

Silence stood bravely between them.

After a few moments had passed, Stephen reached for Natasha's hand. "I'm sorry, Tasha. I don't know what's gotten into me. But I promise, I'm over it."

Natasha looked up at him, her face was as blank as the mustard-colored lunchroom wall in front of them.

"I was really being a jerk," Stephen said, his eyes resting on his lap. "I'm sorry for putting so much pressure on you. Can you forgive me?" Stephen met Natasha's eyes, sincerity oozing from them.

Natasha smiled. "Of course."

Conscious of their surrounding, they hugged briefly.

"So prom is Friday night? Are we going?"

"I don't have a dress. Everything's probably going to be picked over by now."

"I know whatever you find, you'll look beautiful. I've got a special night planned for us."

Natasha offered a curious smile. "Oh really, what do you have in mind?"

"You'll just have to wait until Friday night."

Chapter 18

Brittany couldn't wait for the school day to end. It wasn't just a figment of her imagination, she had become a social outcast. Hushed conversations were neatly constructed behind her back but close enough to signify she was the subject. Early that day, she was walking past a group of boys when one of them shouted out, "Better not ask her to prom, dawg, you'll get locked up!" The whole group broke out in laughter.

When her mother finally pulled up in front of the school, Brittany hurried to the car and plunked down in the front seat. Her mother smiled. "That's a cute outfit. I don't remember buying it."

Brittany's eyes nearly popped out of her head. She looked down at her cute jean outfit. She had forgotten to change her clothes before the end of the school day. "Oh, Natasha bought this for me in France," she said, searching out the window for some way to quickly change the subject. "Mom, I have something I need to talk to you about."

"Yes, dear?"

"The senior prom's next week and no one has asked me to go. Do you think it's because of what happened?"

"No, of course not. Your generation is much different than mine. You guys don't seem to make a big deal about the school dances. In my day, we got all dressed up and went with our dates. You guys go in groups. This is the first I've heard you mention your prom. I assumed you weren't interested in going. Are your friends going?"

"Yes, everybody's going." Brittany let out an exaggerated huff. "It's the senior prom for chrissake!"

"Dear, calm down," her mother pleaded. "Why don't I put a call into Dr. and Mrs. Nesbitt. Maybe their son wouldn't mind escorting you."

"Ugh, he's a dork! Forget it! I just won't go."

"I think Raymond's cute," Brittany's mom said with a hopeful tone. "Besides, if you miss your senior prom, you'll regret it the rest of your days."

"Hmphf!"

Her mother sighed. "Well, it's up to you. I know I would have hated to miss mine."

Brittany held her tongue, but she really wanted to tell her mother that high school had been her glory days and she needed to let them go and quit trying to hold on to her high school experience. It's over! Brittany sucked on her teeth. Then she recalled that Raymond did have a cute 'lil BMW. "Fine. Call. But don't tell them that I'm asking. Tell them my date came down with the chickenpox or something."

When mother and daughter arrived home, Brittany's dad's car was parked directly in front of the door. This usually signified that he was making a quick stop, then leaving again. When they entered the house, her father was standing at the door, waiting to pounce on an intruder with the intensity of a pit bull. Her mother walked toward him and greeted him gently with a kiss on the lips, but he never took his eyes off his daughter. "Hey babe, what are you doing home so early?" Brittany's mom said.

"Well, I came home to get some business papers, but I was thumbing through the mail, when I found this," her dad said, whipping out a sheet of paper from underneath his arm.

Mrs. Brown reached for it and studied the bill. Brittany could see the bold green symbol of the credit card company. Her heart raced as she looked helpless between her father's angry stare and her mother's disappointment. Mr. Brown pushed his glasses back on the bridge of his nose. "You want to tell us what this is?"

Brittany shrugged. Playing stupid would be her best defense, she thought.

"Brittany!" his voice boomed through the house. Her dad never raised his voice.

"I'm sorry, Dad."

"Sorry for what?"

"I'm sorry about the card."

"No, you are sorry you got caught. We told you before you left that we didn't have the money and to use the card only for an emergency."

"I did. All that stuff I bought was on sale and I knew I wouldn't be back over there until the fall and all the sales would be over. I thought you would have been proud of me. I didn't pay full price for anything."

"You hear this, Sheila?" Brittany's dad said. "You've created a monster."

"Oh no you don't, Albert, don't put that on me."

Brittany's parents went back and forth for quite awhile. The argument was centered around money. Mrs. Brown's voice was shaky. "Everyone's suffering because you decided you wanted to build your own medical facility. I can't get my hair done but every two weeks. I haven't been shopping in months. Brittany can't go away to college." Her mother continued naming all the ways their family's lifestyle was changing. "What's next, Albert? Are we going to have to move out of our home?"

Brittany saw the tears in her mother's eyes, but she couldn't console her. Her mind was still on the fact that she would not be going away to college. How could they do that to her? That was like a death sentence. She had spent all that money on applications fees to Duke, UNC, Syracuse and Northwestern. She had been accepted to all of her choice schools. The application to Emory, which her brother Kevin attended, she had crumpled up and thrown it in the garbage, along with the money order. The sound of her dad's voice snapped her back to reality. "You, young lady, upstairs!"

Brittany turned around to look at her mother. "Mom, are you still going to call the Nesbitts about the prom?"

Brittany's dad offered a look that could have rendered her headless had his eyes been two machetes. "There will be no prom for you. Absolutely not!"

"Please, daddy, it's the senior prom. You can take the money out of my savings account."

"You don't have enough to cover this bill. Get a newspaper and start looking for a job! You are going to pay me back for this. And if you wanted to go to the prom, maybe you should have thought about the consequences and repercussions of your actions before you did something so stupid and immature." He turned his attention to his wife. "Sheila, this is your fault. Our daughter takes after you!"

Brittany hurried upstairs so quickly, she almost fell. Her parents were in an all-out battle and she was caught in the middle. Normally, they never argued, but money was obviously a hot button for them. She slipped into her tattered Tweety Bird slippers and stretched out on the bed. There was no way she was going to stay in the house another year with them. Her parents were going to kill her if they found out that she had never turned in her application to Emory. Her thoughts were everywhere. She lay in bed thinking for hours until she couldn't think anymore. And she still hadn't come up with a solution to her problems. But no matter what, she was definitely not staying in the house with her parents another year. The DeKalb County jail looked more suitable than her parents' prison.

Chapter 19

When Shaniqua arrived home, the house was quiet which meant the nurse probably couldn't stay late as she did some nights when Shaniqua had to work. All day, Shaniqua kept thinking about Fabrianna. Brittany's sarcastic remarks lingered in her mouth like sour vomit. No matter what she ate or drank, she just couldn't get rid of the bad taste. She just kept repeating Brittany's words, "There are plenty of nice people in the world, that doesn't mean that you have to go out with them." Shaniqua was so confused. She needed to talk with someone. Though her grandmother was old and didn't always understand, Granny had a unique way of viewing the world, she tapped softly on the bedroom door. "Granny, you up?"

Seconds passed quietly. Deciding against waking up her grandmother, she returned to the kitchen and opened a can of chicken noodle soup for dinner. Her thoughts were on Fabrianna. She wondered if maybe she was confusing friendship with romantic feelings. When she finished her tasteless canned soup, she tried to study her notes, but she was just too exhausted. She felt as though she was carrying the weight of the world on her shoulders. So many decisions had to be made about her future. Would she go to college? Would she leave Granny in the care of someone else? Was she really gay? The phone interrupted. The caller ID showed Fabrianna's number. Every night Fabrianna called to make sure she had made it safely in from school or work. Shaniqua didn't really want to talk until she had a chance to sort through her thoughts and feelings, but if she didn't answer Granny was sure to complain. "Hello."

"Hey, how are you?"

"Fine," Shaniqua replied.

"How was your day?"

"Fine."

"Did you get your prom dress yet?"

"No, I didn't have a chance."

"What's wrong with you?"

"Nothing. I'm just tired. Can we talk tomorrow?"

"What's the matter with you?"

"Nothing, Fabrianna, I'm just really tired."

"Sure thing, we'll talk tomorrow. Good night."

Without warning, a headache seized Shaniqua's head, squeezing it until she thought her brain would pop. She slammed her books closed, took two aspirin and made her way upstairs to bid Granny goodnight. She tapped on the door, "Granny, may I come in?"

No answer. Only the constant hum from the fan mounted in the small window. She pushed the bedroom door. It creaked open. Granny was lying so still, it was unnerving. Shaniqua rushed to the side of the bed, but her grandmother was still motionless. Granny's chest was not rising. Shaniqua could hear her own heart beating. Tears quickly filled her eyes. She reached for the telephone and dialed 9-1-1. As soon as the operator answered, Shaniqua screamed, "My grandmother's not breathing! I need help. Please someone help me." She cradled her grandmother in her arms like a baby and didn't let go until the paramedics burst through the door. "We need you to come out," one of the paramedics ordered.

The other paramedic checked her breathing and then ripped her grandmother's dress in two. Shaniqua fingers were so shaky she could barely dial her Aunt Kathy's telephone number. "Granny's had another attack. The paramedics are here now," she cried. As soon as she finished giving Kathy what little information she had, she left a frantic voice message on Natasha's phone. She clung to the doorway of Granny's bedroom watching.

"One, two, three, four, five," the heavy-set paramedic said and dove in, placing his mouth her grandmother's. Then he began the chest compressions again. He worked like that for a few minutes while the other worker placed tiny square patches all around her grandmother's chest. The heart defibrillator hummed away.

Moments later, Aunt Kathy's voice echoed throughout the house, "Momma?"

Suddenly, the room drew quiet. Within seconds, one of the paramedic's emerged with a grim look. Shaniqua immediately understood the sadness in his eyes. Her lips quivered, but no words came out. Her heart plunged out of her body, collapsing her in the doorway. Tears poured out of her, from deep within her soul. The only love she had ever truly known was leaving her, allowing emptiness to fill her with pockets of nothingness. She began screaming and crying hysterically. She crawled to the bed on legs that seemed broken and draped her thin body over her grandmother's bare chest. She buried her face into her grandmother's cold one. Her voice was barely audible as she whispered in her grandmother's ear, begging and pleading. "Granny, don't leave me. Please don't leave me. I need you. Granny, don't leave me. Granny, Granny, please, don't! I'll do anything, just don't leave me here. Take me with you, Granny, please. Please."

Sometime that evening, when Shaniqua awoke, she could hear the voices of a house full of people. She didn't remember even going to bed. She must have fainted and maybe one of her uncles carried her to her bed. When the sting from the dry contacts lenses became unbearable, she removed the hazel-colored contacts, accidentally ripping one of them. Without alerting anyone downstairs, she threw the lenses on the bathroom floor and took to her bed once more. The weight of reality came crushing down on her once again. She drew her body in a tight ball, where it was safe from all hurt, harm and danger, and cried herself into oblivion.

Chapter 20

For three days, Shaniqua didn't get out of bed. She couldn't eat. She didn't want to shower. The same sweat-stained clothes hung raggedly on her body. The pain wouldn't allow her to even talk to her best friends. She had turned off her cell and refused to answer the house phone. The only person in the world she wanted to talk to, she could never talk to again. Her bedroom provided the only comfort there was in the world. It was her sanctuary.

Mid-morning, Shaniqua was stretched out across the bed when she heard yet another car pull up in front of her grandmother's house. So many people had been streaming in and out the house all day long, offering condolences, gathering Granny's clothes to take to the funeral home, all of which she couldn't allow herself to take part in. It was too final. The doorbell sounded. Shaniqua lay there and pretended like she had been doing for days—that she was not there. Whoever it was could come inside, get what they needed and leave.

"Shaniqua!" a familiar voice bellowed.

Shaniqua crammed the pillows over her head to tune

out her best friend. Moments later, there was a tapping at the door. She lay there quiet and motionless, hoping her friend would turn away. The bedroom door creaked open. "Hey girl," Natasha said softly.

Brittany surveyed the room. Posters held the peeling eggshell color on the wall. Small piles of clothes were scattered about. She had never actually been inside Shaniqua's bedroom. Brittany's eyes traveled to a large lump in the bed. "Shaniqua?"

The room was deafly quiet. Natasha and Brittany passed worried looks.

"Hey, it's me, Brittany super-delicious-will-give-you-a-toothache-if-you-look-at-this-eye-candy-too-long Brown."

Natasha rolled her eyes at Brittany. Suddenly, Shaniqua rose up with a slight grin on her face. "Only you, Brit, only you!"

"Hey, it worked!" Brittany said, wrapping her arms around Shaniqua. "Give me a hug."

Natasha took a seat on the other side of Shaniqua and squeezed tightly. "How's my girl?"

Shaniqua looked up through swollen, dark eyes and shrugged.

Brittany cupped her face in her hands. "So, this is what you look like without contacts. Your eyes are pretty. Why do you have to wear them crazy looking things all the time?"

Natasha's mouth fell open. "Brittany, shut up!"

"Girl, it's okay. I'm used to this crazy nut by now." Shaniqua smiled. "I gave up paying Brittany any attention back in freshman year."

Brittany smiled back. "You know you my girl, right?"

Shaniqua nodded.

"How are you doing?" Natasha asked.

Shaniqua looked down in her lap and studied the lines in her denim jeans. Brittany had been a good distraction for the moment. The pain ballooned deep inside her and forced tears to surface without warning. "It hurts, Tasha. It hurts so bad. I don't know what I'm going to do."

Brittany and Natasha both held their friend tightly. "We're here for you, girl. Don't worry," Natasha said, while Brittany nodded her agreement.

"I don't know where I'm going to live."

"Well, you can always become imprisoned at the Brown compound."

Shaniqua smiled through tear-stained eyes.

"Girl, we'll figure it all out together. Seriously, I'm here for you," Natasha said, rubbing Shaniqua's back. "Let's just take one step at a time. And right now, we're getting you out of the house. Let's go eat!"

"Yeah, them lil' bones need all the meat they can get."

"Shut up, Brittany!" Shaniqua retorted.

"That's my girl! I knew I could pull it out of you. Alright, now go take a shower." Brittany wiped at her nose. "I'm not trying to be funny but you know. You know!"

"Shut up, Brittany!" Shaniqua and Natasha chimed.

Chapter 21

Rain pounded against the pavement as Shaniqua rode in the passenger seat of her cousin Nee Nee's car. Puddles of rainwater gathered at street corners, waiting. Waiting for the sun to dry up everything, make it better, new. Yet, the sun would never be able to help her make it better, dry up her pain. The raw pain of loneliness was searing inside her, ripping her insides out and no one could help. Everyone had tried. Aunt Kathy, Nee Nee, Dorothy Mae, Pastor Cosby, Natasha and even, Brittany. They had all tried. Tried and failed miserably.

Dark clouds hovered in the sky as Shaniqua stepped out of the car. She couldn't believe she was actually getting ready to bury her grandmother, bury the only person who ever loved her. With her nerves cinched deeply in her stomach, she entered the church for the first time ever without her grandmother.

The small church was packed, standing room only. In a room of over three hundred people, Shaniqua found comfort in Natasha's and Brittany's faces. She offered a slight smile to their families and made her way to the front to have a seat in the reserved row. All of her family was there. She had heard that her mother was in town, but she had been dodging her. Her mother and her aunt Kathy had taken care of the funeral arrangements.

Pastor Cosby acknowledged their presence with a warm nod and then carried on about how God was calling one of his good Shepherds home. Quiet anger was brewing underneath Shaniqua's vacant eyes. She wanted the whole church to leave, taking their stupid remarks with them of how God needed her grandmother more. Not even God could comfort her now. Her only thoughts were of how she could join her grandmother.

That evening after the funeral, Shaniqua returned to Nee Nee's house while the rest of the family gathered at her Aunt Kathy's house. Shaniqua had begged Nee Nee to let her come over. She couldn't stand the thought of going back to the empty townhouse or worse, meeting up with her mother at Aunt Kathy's house. With so many things to ponder, she craved alone time. She had to sort out her life. Where would she go now?

Shaniqua was stretched out on the couch with her eyes closed when Nee Nee came out of her bedroom and plopped down at the other end of the sofa. A cloud of smoke followed her and was now swirling between them.

Shaniqua hadn't realized that Nee Nee had come home. The smell in the air was that of burning, sweet grass. "You want a hit?" Nee Nee offered. "It'll make you feel a whole lot better?"

Before Shaniqua realized it, her thin lips were wrapped around the joint, drawing a long, deep drag. Nee Nee had poured her a drink and within minutes, they were laughing at all the funny things that Granny had done. Like the time Granny chased Nee Nee around the dining room table with a switch for digging into a freshly baked apple pie. Shaniqua remembered the time her grandmother had fallen on a piece of ice one winter and landed on all fours, and she and Nee Nee had thought it was the funniest thing in the world. They laughed so hard until they nearly wet their pants and Granny threatened to get a switch.

They sat on the couch munching on chips and laughing away the tears until the doorbell rang. Nee Nee swung open the apartment door. "Hey, Auntie."

"Hey niece, what's happenin'?" Karen hugged Nee Nee and immediately recognized the pungent smell. She scurried over to her daughter who was carelessly sprawled on the couch. "What the hell are you doin'?"

"What do you care?"

"What do you mean, what do I care? I care a whole hell of a lot."

"Karen, please. Don't even try to come here and play mother now. You should of thought about that fifteen years ago."

"Girl, I'll slap the taste out yo' damn mouth, call me Karen again."

Shaniqua rolled her eyes heavenward. Only God knew all the things that she wanted to tell her mother. How she was a "sorry-ass excuse" for a mother and an even sorrier excuse for a daughter. What kind of daughter would deliberately steal her own mother's rent money and then have the nerve to show up at her funeral like she really loved and cared about her. Shaniqua shot her mother a look of pure hatred.

Karen drew in a long, deep breath. "Babygirl," her voice softened as she placed her peeling faux leather purse down on the couch. "I know you're hurting. We all are. But that ain't no excuse to start using drugs. You want to end up like me? Huh?" Karen said, taking a seat next to Shaniqua. "You think I thought I was going to become a dope fiend and alcoholic when I took my first hit and drink in high school? No. But see that's how it always starts out—all fun and games and the next minute you're hooked and ain't a damn thing you can do about it. Or anyone else for that matter."

Shaniqua studied the floor. She had no desire to look at Karen. She hated her even more now.

"Renee, why in the hell did you give Shaniqua that shit?"

"Auntie, that girl's damn near grown. I guess you forgot, you and mom let me smoke with y'all and I was only fourteen," Nee Nee replied.

The tension was thick. Karen was quiet. Maybe she was reflecting back on her niece's statement for truth. Using her dark, bony fingers, she made an effort to smooth down her woolly hair. Shaniqua stood up and grabbed her sweater from the back of the couch. "Where

141

you goin'?" Karen snapped.

Shaniqua whipped her head around. "Why do you care? You ain't been caring."

"Look, Shaniqua, your grandmother's gone. And ain't nothing I can do to bring her back," Karen said adamantly. "So, I'm in charge of you."

"Like hell! Shaniqua said, rushing toward the door. "I don't want to see you ever again. I hate you! You ain't my mother and never have been!" she screamed. All the pain that she kept buried inside for years came roaring out. With tears so thick, she could barely see through them. "I hate you! I hate you! Just because you get on drugs and alcohol or whatever the hell you were doing, doesn't give you the right to just forget about me. What about me? I was only five when you left. How could you do that to me? Huh, how?"

"I came back to check on you from time to time."

Shaniqua stared at her mother. Mother and daughter had the same sad eyes, same hollow expression. Shaniqua wiped her tears with the bottom of her black dress. She breathed in deeply, relieved that the pain was out. Her mother would never understand the hurt she had caused her. Maybe she never wanted to understand it. Shaniqua quietly opened the door and eased out into the rain.

Before she knew what was happening, she dialed

Natasha's number. She needed a friend. The ache of loneliness mushroomed inside, filling every crevice. She didn't know where to turn or who to turn to. She had never felt so alone in the world. Time had ticked down to nothingness. She didn't know how long she spent on the phone with her friend, talking and crying. Suddenly she found herself pushing the heavy door open to enter her grandmother's house; the familiar scent of mothballs greeted her. Granny loved to put mothballs in all the closets.

She went into the dining room and sank down into the old sofa that felt like arms cradling her when she heard a car pull up in front of the house. The engine was as loud as a racing engine. She peeked out of the living room window, Granny style, ducking her head from behind the heavy brown curtain. It was Fabrianna. Shaniqua quickly ducked back as she heard the car door slam. Her mind was racing, should she answer the door? If she did answer it, then she would be forced to talk to Fabrianna. The truth is she really didn't have anything to say. The doorbell sounded. Shaniqua stalled by the window, still trying to decide what to do. The doorbell sounded a second time. Without ever recognizing it, her feet carried her to the door. "Yes?"

"Hey girl, it's me."

Shaniqua swung the door open. "Hey," she said her voice barely audible.

"What's up, I've been trying to get in touch with you for days. How come you haven't returned my calls?"

Shaniqua heard the anger in Fabrianna's voice even though she kept it low and steady. "My grandmother passed away and I just didn't feel like talking to anyone."

"Ohmigod!" Fabrianna said, reaching to wrap her arms around Shaniqua. "Why didn't you say something sooner? When's the funeral?"

"We buried her today."

"What!" Fabrianna shook her head. "Why didn't you tell me? I would have wanted to be there for you. Are you okay?"

Shaniqua shrugged.

Suddenly, Fabrianna turned up nose. "Have you been drinking alcohol and smoking weed?"

Shaniqua shrugged her shoulders nonchalantly. "You wanted to know about my mother, well, she's a dope fiend and an alcoholic!"

"So you want to be one too?"

The silence between them was deafening.

"Come on, Shaniqua. I know you are better than that. Drugs and alcohol ain't never the answer."

"So don't nobody care about me. Who gives a damn about what Shaniqua Williams does?" Tears ripped through her, to the point where she was barely understandable. "The only somebody that ever gave a damn about me is dead. She's gone. She's gone forever. My granny is gone. I don't know who the hell my dad is. My momma didn't love me enough to stick by me. Only my granny." Her face was dripping with wetness. Fabrianna held her so close, hugging her until the sobbing subsided. "What am I going to do now? Where will I go? I'm not even eighteen yet."

"Well, you will be in a few weeks. Can you stay with your cousin until then?"

"Maybe, and then what?"

The silence was so complete.

Shaniqua gently pushed away from her friend. "Look, I want to be alone right now."

Fabrianna studied Shaniqua for a few moments. "Just promise me you aren't going to do any more drugs."

Shaniqua looked at her without responding.

"I'm serious, girl. How do you think your grandmother would feel if she knew what you had done?"

"Fabrianna, would you please leave? I want to be alone."

"Cool. I only came by to ask you if you decided about prom yet? Tomorrow's the last day to buy the tickets."

A mean feeling came stealing over Shaniqua like she didn't care if she hurt anyone's feelings. She had pondered that event from every angle and each time she came up with the same conclusion, she definitely didn't want to go to prom as a gay couple. She scanned the room for something to focus on other than Fabrianna's intense dark eyes. The floor was a willing participant. The worn out hardwood stared back. Shaniqua drew in a deep breath. "Look, Fabrianna, I don't think I'm gay."

"But how do you know?"

Shaniqua frowned. "What do you mean how do I know?" she snapped. "I know because I've never been gay. I've never thought about being with another girl before. Don't most real gay people say that they've been that way all their life? Plus, I want to have kids some day."

"Gay people can have kids."

"Granny said 'that two like people, don't make a right society.'"

Fabrianna scrunched her face. "What?"

"Never mind, I'm just not interested." Shaniqua stood up and started for the door. "I think you're cool and all, and I'm not judging you, but I'm not trying to be down like that," she said, holding the door open.

Fabrianna grimaced. "All right, later!"

"Yep, later!" Shaniqua slammed the door shut and collapsed on the new sofa. Bone-crushing loneliness filled her. With tears trickling down the sides of her face, she began to ponder the meaning of life. Her life. A life without Granny. Who would she live with? Would she go to college? After hours of grieving, she packed her clothes and phoned Nee Nee to come pick her up. There was no way she was going to stay in the townhouse without her grandmother.

Chapter 22

All week Natasha kept busy preparing for the prom. She had found the perfect dress at the last minute, a sleek red gown with a gorgeous plunging neckline. She convinced her mom that the gown was appropriate and promised to wear a safety pin across the bosom to prevent revealing too much cleavage. As she dressed for the prom, she felt herself growing more enthusiastic, but not nearly as excited as Stephen. He had been talking about it nonstop the entire week, carrying on about how much fun they were going to have and how this was going to be the most special night for them.

She was dusting her face with a light, translucent powder when she heard a knock on the door. Suddenly her mother bulldozed her way in. Sometimes she wondered why she even bothered to close her door. No one seemed to respect her privacy, especially her brothers.

"Hey sweet pea, oh my, don't you look beautiful. God, you look so grown up. Where did the time go?" Her mom took a seat and looked as though she was really trying to track it.

The satin red bodice gown looked elegant on Natasha's long, slender frame. Her hair was swept up in a purposely messy updo, chandelier earrings dangled from her earlobes. Natasha smiled at herself in the full-length mirror. She had successfully pulled her look together at the last minute. There was no doubt in her mind that she was going to be the talk of the prom. Now, she actually was glad that Stephen convinced her to go. Hopefully, Shaniqua would be there, too. Yes, she would miss Brittany there, but they would have a lifetime of parties to enjoy together. But then again, her mom always said, "After high school, people change. They go their separate ways." As Natasha slid into her stilettos, she wondered if that would really happen to them. *Definitely not! They were always going to remain friends.*

"Sweet pea, we need to talk."

Natasha raised her perfectly plucked brow at her mother's request. Her tone was much too serious. "Mom, what is it? Stephen will be here any minute."

"This is important. He can wait."

An exaggerated huff escaped from her lips. Natasha was sure it could wait until tomorrow. Jeez!

Her mom patted the area next to her on the bed gesturing for Natasha to sit. "Sweet pea, I know we've talked about sex before, but . . ."

Natasha's mind quickly combed over her telephone conversations with Stephen. Had she been eavesdropping on another phone? There was no way because she mostly talked to him on her cell. Maybe her mom had stood outside her bedroom door, listening.

". . . there are a few things I think we should talk

about."

The sound of her mother's voice snapped her back to the present.

"As your dad and I have always told you, there's nothing new under the sun. I know what young people have on their minds on prom night."

Natasha remained straight-faced. She was not going to give her mother any indication that she was right.

"There are several reasons why young people don't need to have sex."

She glared at the clock sitting on her nightstand. "Mom, I already know."

"I know you know, but I want to say it again just in case you may have forgotten."

"I didn't forget!"

"Stop interrupting me. Young people, not just girls, but boys too, don't need to have sex because most young people are not mentally, emotionally and oftentimes physically, responsible. I know you guys think you're ready because your hormones are working overtime. But believe me, you are not ready. I've been where you are, so don't think I don't know what I'm talking about."

Natasha wanted to ask her mom badly when was the first time she had sex? Was it with her dad? She had done the math. Her parents were married the same year that her oldest brother, Nate, was born, which meant that her mother was approximately three months pregnant when she married her father. Her dad had just graduated college, but her mother had only completed her sophomore year.

"Baby, when a young woman shares herself with a

man, she's giving up a part of herself that leaves her feeling less than whole. You know what I mean?"

Natasha glared at the clock again, then offered a nonchalant nod, but her mother continued talking anyway.

"She will forever be connected to that young man whether it was a good or bad connection. So, sex should ultimately be saved for marriage."

Natasha's thoughts were swelling in her throat. "Did you and Dad wait until marriage?"

Her mom's mouth dropped open. Silence stood between mother and daughter, boldly and defiantly. Slowly, her mother glanced around the room, stalling to collect the truth, or maybe lies. "No. No, we didn't," her mother said, with her gaze fixed on the carpet. "But in a lot of ways, I wished we had. Maybe I would have my college degree now." When she looked at her daughter, it was with eyes full of regret.

Uneasiness was filling the room, every nook and cranny. Natasha remained quiet. She almost felt bad about making her mother admit something so personal. But then again, she was glad that she had asked the question, even though she and her brothers knew the answer. It still felt good to have her mother tell the truth. Parents often held children to certain standards that they themselves weren't able to live up to. Now, Natasha better understood the reasons for her mother wanting her children to obtain college degrees. Her dream had died when Nate was born, even though she had a loving husband.

"Tasha, you'll be eighteen in a couple of months and

you're not going to have daddy and me around to guide you on every decision. I only hope you'll remember the things that we've taught you over the years. Most of all, just know that any guy who isn't willing to wait for you, isn't worth the time of day, and in my momma's words, "Tell him, don't let the door knob hit cha, where the good Lord split cha!"

The doorbell rang. Neil ran upstairs, taking three at a time. "Tasha, Stephen just pulled up in a limo."

"Shut up, boy. Quit playing!"

"For real though!"

Natasha hurried to the window and peeked through the blinds. Her eyes fell on a long, black, sleek limousine. The chauffer looked sophisticated in a black suit standing next to the car door. She hugged her mother before her mother left to greet Stephen downstairs. Natasha was glad they had talked. She was now able to see her mother as a person, not just as her mother. Natasha better understood why her mom was adamant about not repeating mistakes and creating "generational curses," as her mother always said.

Seconds later, she heard her mom and dad downstairs chatting with Stephen. Natasha didn't realize her dad had come over, too. Though she shouldn't have been surprised, he hadn't missed a single event since their divorce. Natasha checked herself from head to toe one last time and blew a kiss in the mirror. *Let the haters hate!* She eased down the stairs with her silver clutch purse tucked neatly under her arm.

Stephen was waiting in the foyer in a black two-button tuxedo. A cherry red vest with a matching tie, made him look very chic, sophisticated like a handsome, male model in a tuxedo advertisement. When he noticed Natasha, his lips curled into a soft smile. "Wow! Tasha."

She blushed.

"Let me get my camera," Natasha's mother said, dashing into the kitchen. She returned immediately. "All right, let's get a picture of you guys. Tasha, put your corsage around your wrist." Natasha cut her eyes at her mom without anyone noticing. Her mom was about to start running everything. She could at least wait until Stephen offered the corsage to her. Stephen gave Natasha an apologetic smile, then opened the plastic container. His fingers were shaky as he secured a beautiful white orchid corsage around her wrist. "All right, stand close together," her mother ordered as if she was directing a motion picture.

Stephen slid his arm around Natasha's waist as they posed for countless pictures. Just when the couple thought the picture-taking session had ended, Natasha's parents escorted them out to the limo to snap more pictures. Embarrassment could not accurately describe how Natasha felt. Her parents were acting brand new like they had never experienced anything before. They both sat inside to inspect the limo, admiring the fancy accent lighting, luxurious black, leather interior and the flat screen television.

As soon as pictures were over, Stephen retreated to one side of the limo while Natasha went to the other. Dressing up had a way of creating formality between couples even if they had been together as long as she and Stephen had. It reminded Natasha of their first date when they went to the movies, Stephen let his knee accidentally brush against hers, and then he didn't move it.

"Alright, Stephen," Mr. Harris said. "I don't have to tell you to take care of my baby girl tonight."

"Yes, sir."

Natasha and Stephen sat side by side in the limo, admiring each other, holding hands while enjoying the romantic environment. When they arrived at the Grand Hotel, some kids were lingering outside smoking. When the limo pulled into the circular driveway, stopping directly in front of the entrance, everyone's heads turned. The chauffeur promptly opened Stephen's door. Stephen stood to the side, held his hand for Natasha to help her ease out of the car. She blushed. This had to be how Cinderella felt in the pumpkin carriage. She looked down at her clear and silver stilettos and giggled to relieve the nervous tension. Too many eyes were on them.

They found their way into the chic Crystal ballroom. High, cathedral style walls greeted them. Large crystal chandeliers dangled from the vaulted ceiling. The tables were elegantly dressed for a five-course meal. Some kids were already on the dance floor, dancing more contained and calmer than usual. Everyone was acting very formal.

Even super ghetto-fabulous Shamauri was trying to act civilized with her black and red striped hair, and powder blue fingernails with a matching skintight dress. Maybe dressing up had away of taming one's behavior, Natasha thought. Other kids were taking pictures with the professional photographer at the back of the ballroom.

She and Stephen took a seat at the back of the room at a table with students they didn't know and saved a place for Shaniqua and Fabrianna in the event they showed up. They dined on grilled chicken with rosemary potatoes while socializing with another couple seated at their table. After dinner, Natasha and Stephen graced the dance floor and didn't get off until she discovered that she was sweating profusely. "Stephen, I'm going to ladies' room. I'll be back." She said and then dashed off.

Once inside, Natasha powdered her face while listening to the girls talk about their plans afterwards. Someone was slumped over a commode, puking. Natasha frowned at the hurling sound. That just didn't make sense to get sloppy drunk. What kind of prom was she going to remember head first in a smelly toilet? Natasha slid on a fresh coat of lip gloss and left the restroom. On the way out, she spotted Adonis standing in the hall talking to a chaperon. Their eyes locked instantly. She couldn't tear her gaze away from him. He was so fine in his a black tuxedo with a white vest and tie. His smile was magnetic drawing her closer into him. "Hi, Adonis."

"What's up, pretty lady? Who you here with, your ball and chain?"

"Anyway. Who are you with?"

"A friend from another school since you wouldn't let

me take you."

"You didn't ask."

"So can I get a dance?"

Excitement rushed her. She quickly hid it behind a healthy dose of attitude. "What about your girlfriend?"

"She's random," Adonis said, with everything on his face curling into a smile—eyelashes, lips, and cheeks. "So will your man mind?"

"No, he's cool," she quickly responded. There was no way she was going to miss the opportunity to dance with Adonis. School was ending soon and this would be one more memory to tuck away in her bank. "Let's go around to the front of the room," she said, hoping that Stephen would still be sitting in the back at their table.

The DJ was spinning the down south rap music and everyone was sweating and getting crunk. Minutes later, the DJ slowed the music. Adonis wrapped his arm around Natasha and pulled her into him. She went easily. His cologne tickled her nose with a clean, fresh fragrance. She was lost in a trance. There was something about him that she instinctively liked. Suddenly, Adonis pulled away from her. Natasha looked up to see what he was doing and found Stephen's angry eyes. Her heart sank. She didn't know what to do. The dance floor had cleared when the slow song came on. Only six couples were on the floor.

"What's up with this?" Stephen said, his tone razor sharp.

"Dude, you better step off," Adonis said, taking a step back.

Natasha looked at Adonis in his ready-to-swing-on-a-brotha stance. Stephen looked like he was ready to go the distance, too. She swallowed so hard, she wondered if her tongue was still in her mouth. She didn't want them to fight over her, not to mention mess up everyone's prom forever. Suddenly, Adonis took a step forward closer to Stephen. "So what's up, what you wanna do?"

She slid her body between them to prevent them from coming to blows. "Wait, guys, it's not that serious. Stephen, Adonis and I were just dancing. It's nothing to it."

"Yeah, you better school that fool!" Adonis said.

"Come on, Adonis. Chill," Natasha said, looking at Adonis with pleading eyes that Stephen couldn't see.

"It's cool," Adonis said, slowly taking steps backwards. "Tasha, I'll holla."

She glared at her boyfriend through angry eyes. "Stephen, why'd you do that?"

"You're supposed to be my date. Let him get his own."

Natasha frowned and walked back to the table, biting back the desire to throw Keisha up in his face again. She just didn't need the drama on prom night. There were so many horror stories out there, and she was not going to be the one everyone talked about Monday morning in school. She hoped no one witnessed the exchange. She put on a happy face and tried to relax at the table until the dance was over, but her thoughts were on Adonis. Maybe she didn't really need to be in a committed relationship, she thought. She liked Stephen, but the truth was, she liked Adonis, too.

Chapter 23

When the prom was over, Stephen and Natasha made their way to their limo. A few other limousines were waiting outside the hotel, but groups of kids piled into them. Natasha smiled—her situation was different, more romantic. Once they were seated inside, Stephen rolled down the black divider to speak to the chauffeur. "To the Hyatt, please."

Those words bounced back and forth in Natasha's head like a game of ping-pong. Previous conversations with Stephen about prom night filled her mind. They had talked about getting a room months ago, but then never discussed it again. She wondered where he had gotten the money for both the limousine and an upscale hotel room.

The hotel lobby was beautifully decorated in rich earth tones, warm oranges and vibrant reds. The piano bar was crowded with adults. Natasha's thoughts immediately went to Brittany and how she had rocked the crowd last year at her sweet sixteen party with Alicia Keys' "Fallin'". Natasha relaxed a little when she observed other prom couples wandering about the hotel. Although, she didn't recognize any of them because they were from different schools, it was reassuring to know that she wasn't the only one out there.

They took the glass elevator to the fifteenth floor where Stephen asked Natasha to wait outside their hotel room. With her feet throbbing, she waited for what seemed like an eternity. She wondered what Stephen was doing and why she couldn't go in. After a couple of minutes, Stephen swung the door open and led Natasha inside the room. Several white vanilla scented candles lit the elegant room, casting a warm glow. Natasha smiled; she had never thought of Stephen as the romantic type. In fact, she could count the number of times that she had received flowers from him on one finger. And that was for Sweetest day. Her eyes stole over to the bed. A king-size bed with fluffy, oversized pillows. Normally beds looked comfortable, but this one looked intimidating, like it was going to come alive and suck her in if she sat down. Natasha took a seat in the chair next to the window. The view was magnificent. Beautiful lights illuminated all of downtown Atlanta.

"Tasha, get comfortable and I'll be back in a minute," he said, then dashed into the bathroom.

With nothing else to do, she reached for the remote

and channel surfed. When he returned, he gently removed the remote from her grasp and turned off the television. He then walked to the other side of the room and turned on the radio. She watched him closely, witnessing the nervousness in his step. Sweat clang to his once crisp white shirt, gluing it to his back. She looked down at her watch. "Stephen, how are we going to get home? I have to be back by two o'clock."

"Don't worry, my dad's car is parked downstairs."

Stephen motioned for Natasha to come have a seat next to him at the foot of the bed. She gladly kicked off her shoes, but she didn't want to get too comfortable—it would send the wrong message. She toyed with the ring Stephen had given her right before their last breakup; a cute, heart-shaped ring. She smiled. Her boyfriend was a really sweet guy.

Suddenly, he sandwiched her hand between his hands. "Tasha, I know this is going to sound corny, but I just want you to know how . . . I mean." He drew in a deep breath to calm his nerves. "What I really want to say is, I love you, Tasha. You mean the world to me."

She gazed into his hazel eyes. They were so soft and sincere looking. There was no doubt that his feelings were real. They had built their relationship on the foundation of friendship nearly two years ago. "Stephen, I love you, too."

He leaned in for a kiss. She met his lips with hers. They were kissing so passionately, she became lost in oblivion while time ticked away freely. She didn't even know how long she had been lying on her back. Everything felt so good and wonderful. Her body was experiencing new sensations when suddenly he gently tugged at her dress to undo the zipper. When Natasha realized what was happening, she stopped kissing, raised herself up and gently pushed him away. "Stephen, the time isn't right."

"What do you mean? We have a whole hour."

She cut her eyes at him for thinking so narrow-mindedly. Her thoughts raced back to her mom's words, "Sometimes, men and boys have only one thing on their minds. So it's up to you to be the strong one." She and Stephen were sitting close. "I'm not ready to go down that road yet. I want to at least wait until I'm eighteen and out of high school."

"Tasha, we'll be out of high school in two weeks. The time is perfect."

"No, it's not just that." She stood up and left him sitting on the bed. "I don't want to be pressured into it."

"I'm not pressuring you."

"No, what I'm saying is, when the time is right, I won't feel guilty about it. I don't want to hide it from my parents."

"So you want to be married?"

"I don't even know if I'll ever get married. Marriages don't seem to work," Natasha snapped. Before she realized it, tears had surfaced in her eyes. Even though her parents got along well, they were still divorced. To this day, she still didn't know what happened and neither of them seemed interested in discussing it.

Stephen reached up to wipe a tear that had traveled to the bottom of her chin. "I'm sorry. This is about your parents, isn't it?"

"Yes, no. I mean. I don't know what I mean."

"Tasha, I'm here for you. I'm not going anywhere. We'll be together. Watch." Stephen started kissing her on the neck.

"I'm still not ready, though," Natasha said, abruptly moving away from him. "I want to go home."

"Fine."

Separated by a stonewall of silence, they rode in the car with the music at full volume.

Chapter 24

Sunday morning, the split of daylight crept through the dusty mini-blinds in Nee Nee's apartment. When Shaniqua awoke, she instinctively sat up. There was no smell of Granny's flapjacks or crispy fried bacon floating through the house—their Sunday ritual. Only the smell of Nee Nee's Money Green incense lingering from the night before. She looked down at her large face watch. It was only 5:45 a.m., the time she usually awoke for the sunrise service. She threw her body against the black leather sofa and pulled the covers over her head. Church wouldn't see her today or probably ever. What God had done was cruel. He knew that her grandmother was the only somebody that ever loved her. A tear trickled out the corner of her eye, meshing into her bushy hairline.

She didn't know how long she had been asleep when she heard Nee Nee coming through the front door. "What time is it?" Shaniqua asked.

"Ten-thirty."

"I thought you said you'd be home around seven-thirty."

Nee Nee pursed her lips. "I had to take care of something after the club closed. Damn! My own momma don't sweat me," Nee Nee snapped. "Don't come over here with that Granny shit now!"

Shaniqua scrunched her face in confusion.

"I don't need no damn body judging what the hell I do."

Shaniqua meekly shook her head, refusing to get into a verbal confrontation with her cousin. It's not like she had anywhere else to lay her head. She couldn't go to her Aunt Kathy's house because her mother was probably staying there until she ventured off again. Moreover, Granny never allowed Shaniqua to go over there because of the company Aunt Kathy liked to keep. Granny always said, "A bunch of men friends over your chil'ren ain't right."

Suddenly there was a knock at the door. Shaniqua quickly grabbed her shoes and blanket, and tiptoed into the bathroom. "If that's Karen, tell her I'm not here," she said, ducking into the shower.

Nee Nee looked out the peephole and then down at herself in white thigh high boots. She opened the door halfway. "Hey, Pastor," she said, hiding behind the door.

"Mornin' Renee," he said, standing there in a well-fitted, dark suit. "How you doin'?"

"Fine," she said, smiling, her gold front tooth reflecting the light.

"When are you going to come back?" he said, making his way into the apartment. "Our choir would love to have you again."

Nee Nee shrugged.

"It's never too late to turn your life around. God loves us all, sinners and saints alike. Remember that."

Nee Nee closed the apartment door and yelled, "Come on out, it's Pastor Cosby."

Shaniqua emerged slowly from the bathroom. "Hey Pastor."

"Just the person I wanted to see. We missed you at service this morning."

She offered a slow and methodical nod, but said nothing.

"Shaniqua, I'd like to talk to you for a moment," he said, taking a seat on the couch.

Nee Nee gladly retreated into the bedroom while Shaniqua sat down on the opposite end of the couch.

"I know what you're going through." A long pause held the moment. "I know you think I don't, but I do. I've been where you are."

Shaniqua still refused to look at him. She already knew everything he had to say. She had been listening to his sermons all her life.

"I was on my own at fifteen. I had to raise myself. It wasn't until I found the Lord in jail at the age of nineteen, did I begin to turn my life around." Shaniqua fiddled with her fingers. "I want to save you some heartache, if you'll allow me," he said.

She finally let her tear-filled eyes to meet his. "But why did He have to take Granny?" Her voice was clothed in sorrow.

Pastor Cosby scooted down the couch and sat next to her. "I'm not going to pretend to get in God's head. I'm not going to pretend to have all the answers. But there are a few things that I do know. One, I know you were your grandmother's pride and joy. I know she wanted you to make something of yourself, more than she wanted anything in this world. You don't know this, but I think it's time to tell you. Your grandmother had been sick for a very long time. She was doing without her blood pressure medication, just so that she could help provide for you. As soon as the church caught wind of this, we bought her medications every month. But the thing is, we don't know how long she had been sacrificing her health."

Tears cascaded down Shaniqua's pallid face. Pastor Cosby offered his handkerchief. "Don't let all of your grandmother's sacrifices be in vain."

The room was so quiet that the air conditioner kicked on and startled her.

"Shaniqua, you're a very bright young lady. Do you hear what I'm saying to you?"

She nodded.

"Look at me," he said with intense eyes. "The way I see it, you've got two choices. You can stay angry that your grandmother's gone and that you don't have parents or the family life that you've always wanted. Or you can push past this and try to make something of yourself. I don't think I have to tell you what the consequences are. You can look around and see for yourself." He glanced toward Nee Nee's bedroom.

Shaniqua's tears slowly diminished.

"Have you thought about what you want to do with yourself?"

Her shoulders drooped in sadness. "I don't know." Her voice was barely audible. "Maybe nursing."

"A nurse. That sounds great," Pastor Cosby said with enthusiasm. "Well, however the church family can assist you, you let us know. We're here for you. So now, who will you stay with, Renee?"

She nodded.

Pastor Cosby shook his head. "Shaniqua, I don't think that's a good idea. I think she's going to be a negative influence on you. First lady and I want you to come stay with us."

Shaniqua's tears were brimming again.

"I don't mean to upset you. Just think about it and I'll be in touch in a couple of days. Okay?"

She let out periodic burst of sniffles.

"Alright, give me a hug," he said and wrapped her tightly in his warm, safe arms until her tears dried.

As soon as Pastor Cosby left, Shaniqua rushed into Nee Nee's room to talk, but her cousin was sound asleep. There was another knock at the front door. Shaniqua ran to the door thinking Pastor Cosby must have forgotten something and swung the door open. It was her mother. Karen pushed past Shaniqua. "We need to talk."

"There's nothing to talk about," Shaniqua bristled.

"Watch your tone, young lady," her mother said, taking a seat in the same spot where Pastor Cosby had sat. "Now, I know you're hurting, Shaniqua. But we are all each other have."

Shaniqua rolled her eyes.

Karen sighed. "I may not have been the best mother, but I need you to love me for me." A long pause followed. Shaniqua simply stared at the carpet. She wanted to tell Karen that just because someone is your biological parent, doesn't grant them an automatic pass into your heart.

"I want you to come live with me," Karen said, swallowing hard.

Shaniqua scrunched her face. "Live with you where?"

"I live in Baltimore with a nice young man. I think you'll like him. His name's Red."

Her mind raced back to her grandmother. Granny would not approve of this. "No, thanks."

"Well, you don't have the option. I'm still your mother and your legal guardian is deceased."

Shaniqua glared at her mother. "I'll be eighteen in seven weeks and three days. I can make my own decisions." She could tell her mother was taken aback. Maybe she didn't realize just how old she was.

After a quiet moment passed, her mother cleared her throat. "So, what is it you planning on doing?"

"I don't know, but I won't end up like you," she retorted. Silence held the moment. She stared at her mother. Blood shot eyes full of pain stared back at her. She wished she could take the words back, but the fact is it was the truth. She never wanted to end up like her parents. "May I ask you something?" Shaniqua's voice had lost some of its sharpness.

"Go ahead, baby, ask me anything," Karen replied.

"Who's my father?"

The whites of Karen's eyes grew to the size of golf balls. She looked around the room for a response. First, at the floor, then the walls, the kitchen, the leather bar stools in front of the island. After a couple of minutes of awkward silence, Karen found her voice again. "I don't think that's something we should be discussing."

"I'm almost eighteen. I'm a big girl, I can handle it."

Karen clasped her bony dark hands together and placed them between her equally bony legs, which made her kneecaps look oversized. "I don't think that's a good idea."

"I want to know." Shaniqua's voice grew louder and sharper with each word. "And I have a right to know."

Her mother swallowed hard again, then drew in a deep breath and exhaled. "Truth is I don't know your father. He was somebody I met in a bar one night."

"Is he white?"

Her mother nodded.

"What's his name?"

"I can't remember it now."

Tears surfaced without warning. Shaniqua clasped her hands over her eyes. Karen wrapped her arm around her daughter.

Shaniqua quickly pulled away. "Don't touch me. You have a lot of nerve to tell me, 'Just love you for you.' What about me? What about loving me enough to raise me? When you really love somebody, you just don't go off and abandon your child. I waited that day in the hot sun playing jacks until my fingers were raw from scraping the concrete. Granny had to get a switch after me to make me come in the house. Why? Because my mother told me she was going to the corner store to get me a grape tootsie roll pop and you never came back. You never came back!" Tears flooded her vision. "You never came back. You could have at least taken me with you. But you left me. You just left. I was only five years old. How could you do that to me? How? I don't understand," she said. Her voice sounded as though she was five again. A fusion of snot, tears and black mascara covered her face. Using the bottom of her shirt, she wiped her face dry. "So don't tell me we are all each other have!" Her voice was like hot iron. Hard and fiery. "I am all that I have." Shaniqua took a moment to collect her thoughts while her mother offered a blank stare. She swallowed the saliva that had gathered in her mouth as if she was swallowing the pain, then drew in a deep, calming breath before she spoke. Her voice was now steady and composed. "And you know what? I'm going to make the most of it. Have a nice life, because I sure plan to!" she said and bolted for the door, refusing to look again into the eyes of the woman who had caused her so much grief.

Chapter 25

Monday morning when Shaniqua awoke, her thoughts immediately went to her mother. She would be leaving for Baltimore in thirty minutes. She could hear her grandmother's voice, "Shaniqua, that's still yo' momma." And Shaniqua could hear her imaginary response, "Just because she's my biological mother don't mean that's the best option for me." And with that, she dressed and left for school with a sudden burst of enthusiasm. There's no telling how her mother was living and now she knew with certainty that she was still drinking because Nee Nee said they had all gone over to Aunt Kathy's place last night and everyone was drinking.

Shaniqua waited for Brittany and Natasha in the commons area. The gossip was so thick you could have cut it with a knife. Everyone was talking about who did what with whom after the prom, who got stood up and who looked a hot mess. Shaniqua knew better than ever that she had made the right decision not to go with Fabrianna. The students would have had a field day talking about them, too. She could just hear the boys saying, "Y'all are too damn fine. Y'all just ain't had a real man, yet!" She shook the thoughts from her mind and waved Natasha over. She needed to put her own issues behind her. She could hardly wait to hear what happened between Natasha and Stephen. "Girl, where have you been? I called you all day yesterday. Why didn't you answer your phone?"

"What's up, girl? I left my phone on at home by accident and spent the day at my dad's house."

"Well, you could have at least called me from there. Dang, Tasha!"

"I'm sorry girl. How are you holding up?"

Shaniqua offered an apprehensive nod. She had given up trying to put her feelings into words. It only made her cry. Her eyes rested in her lap, her sanctuary. She didn't want to cry. She had to be strong for her grandmother. She remembered what her grandmother always said, "Thinking about others will help you take your mind off your own worries." A slight smile came upon her face and she looked at Natasha. "I want to hear what happened at the prom."

Brittany sashayed her way over. "Hey ladies, what's popping?"

"Tasha was just about to tell me what went down between her and Stephen."

"Nothing went down," Natasha beamed.

Shaniqua slapped her bony hands against her hips. "Tasha, you get on my last nerve frontin'. Now quit playing and tell us."

"First off, I got a bone to pick with you, Ms. Thang," Natasha said, staring at Shaniqua.

"What did I do?"

"You stood me up. Why didn't you tell me that you and Fabrianna weren't coming on Friday? Stephen and I were sandwiched between a bunch of geeks at the dinner table. We were trying to save a space for you. I kept calling you, but you didn't answer your cell."

"Sorry. But I never told you that Fabrianna and I were going."

Brittany giggled. "You did, too!"

"My bad. I had to cut Fabrianna back."

"Oh really," Brittany smirked. "Do tell, inquiring minds want to know."

Shaniqua frowned. "I wasn't down with what she was talking."

Brittany curled her left eyebrow. "Oh really, now."

"Yes, really! She's a nice person, but I'm not gay."

"I'm glad you finally realized that. Half these girls going around here in their little rainbow clique love affairs aren't really gay. Being gay is just a fad, if you ask me. It's like wearing a grill—someone decided it's cool and now everybody and their momma want to do it, too. Brittany Ann Brown ain't going out like a sucka for nobody!"

Natasha smirked. "Thank you, Brittany Ann Brown, but nobody asked you. I really don't think it's just a fad. Some people really are born like that. So live and let die!"

"Whatever!" Brittany sneered. "Well, somebody's going to get their feelings hurt stepping to me sideways."

"Brit, what are you going to do?" Natasha chuckled. "You can't fight!"

Shaniqua slapped Natasha a high-five. "Boo Ya! So, girl,

what's up with you and Stephen? Did y'all go to a hotel?"

"We had a very nice room at the Hyatt."

"Oh, really? Did y'all get down with the get down or what?"

"No, we didn't."

Shaniqua and Brittany passed knowing looks. "Girl, quit lying," Brittany scolded. "She's the sneaky, quiet, shy type who doesn't kiss and tell."

"No, seriously, we didn't. I straight up told him, I wasn't ready," Natasha said earnestly.

Shaniqua frowned. "What are you waiting on? Dang, y'all been going out since Mary and Joseph had Jesus."

"I wasn't feeling him like that."

Brittany smirked. "Well, alrighty then! So are you guys still a couple?"

Natasha shrugged. "Something like that. But Adonis was there looking so good. Hmm, hmm, hmm. The police should have pulled him over and written him a ticket for being too doggone fine!"

The bell rang, summoning them to class.

Brittany chuckled along with her friends. "We'll get to the bottom of this at lunch, ladies."

Natasha moved closer to Shaniqua. "How are you holding up for real, girl?"

Shaniqua shrugged. "I feel like my whole world has been snatched out from underneath me. It's hard, Tasha. I have to decide what I want to do now. I'm going through the world with nobody on my side."

Natasha draped her arm around her friend. "Wrong! You'll always have me. What have I always told you? You're going to always be my girl even if you don't get no bigger than a—?"

Shaniqua smiled. "Squirrel."

"We'll talk some more at lunch. Just know you can always come stay with me and my folks."

"Thanks, Tasha."

Shaniqua moseyed past the guidance counselor's office and without warning, her feet instinctively carried her back to Mrs. Smith's office. History could wait; she had to deal with her future. For the past couple of days, she had tossed around the idea of becoming a nurse. She tapped on the door. Mrs. Smith's curly afro was the first thing Shaniqua saw as she entered her office. "Mrs. Smith, may I come in?"

"Yes. Hi, Shaniqua, how are you?"

"Good. How are you?"

"I'm too blessed to be stressed. God is good all the time. All the time, God is good."

Shaniqua wanted to roll her eyes and say, if he's so good, then why'd He take her grandmother away from her. They say God has a lesson to teach us in everything he does, but where's the lesson in that? Shaniqua grinned to mask her pain.

"What can I do for you?"

"I want to talk with you about college. Mrs. Smith, I

think I want to be a nurse."

A slight smile crept across the guidance counselor's birdlike face. Her beady eyes danced with excitement. "That's great. What's your SAT score?"

"SATs. I didn't take it."

Mrs. Smith gave Shaniqua a cross look. "Ms. Williams, school is going to end in few weeks. Why haven't you already taken the test?"

Shaniqua shrugged. "I guess I wasn't planning on going to college."

"Well, to get admitted anywhere you will need to have taken the SAT or the ACT. Where do you want to go?"

She shrugged once more. "I guess what I really came to talk to you about was how can I afford college. I don't think I'm cut out for the military."

Mrs. Smith grabbed a file off her credenza. "Who said anything about the military? That's one option to go for free, but that's not your only option. Here," she said, handing Shaniqua a pamphlet on financial aid. "All you need to do is fill out this application and mail it in. There's a lot of money out there for disadvantaged students and students of color. And don't let anyone tell you different. Understand?"

"Yes, ma'am."

"Next visit, we'll look at some schools to see which ones have good accredited nursing programs."

Shaniqua looked confused. "Accredited, what's that?"

"You always want to go to a school that has accreditation. Basically, it's validation that the school is a good school. Trust me, I know. I've got three degrees and my husband's a medical doctor."

Shaniqua brightened. She had almost made it out of the office without hearing about her three degrees. "Alright, thanks, Mrs. Smith."

As Shaniqua passed a presentation table on her way out, her eyes landed on a Navy brochure, titled "Accelerate Your Life." Her mind raced to her grandmother's nurse, Ms. Cassandra. She clutched the brochure in her hand and headed to class.

Chapter 26

After school, Brittany waited in the blazing hot sun for her mother to pick her up as usual. She had been very successful in camouflaging the fact that she no longer had her car. She learned to hide out in the girls' bathroom until the school buses pulled away. Her parents never questioned why it took her so long to come out to the car. But this morning was an exception. Her mother had already instructed her to be waiting outside at 3:30 p.m. because she had somewhere to be. Brittany turned to look at the buses when she thought she heard someone calling her name. It was Shaniqua waving her over. Brittany looked around for her mother who was nowhere in sight. "Hey girl," Brittany said.

Shaniqua offered a mischievous smile. "Girl, don't tell me your car is still in the shop."

Brittany nodded.

"Dang, what are they doing, rebuilding it?"

Suddenly, her mother's car rolled slowly toward her. *Saved!* "Girl, I have to go. I'll see you."

Brittany slid into the car, anxious for either her mother to hurry up and pull away or the buses. "Mom, what took you so long? Jeez, I've been waiting out here forever. I've gotten three shades darker."

With smoldering eyes, Mrs. Brown glared at her daughter. "And what's wrong with that?"

Brittany curled her eyebrow and twisted her mouth. She wished she could take the words back. She didn't feel like getting all philosophical about how blacks were still too color struck. She knew that whenever her mother got on the color issue, it was a no-win situation. She had heard that speech more times than she probably heard her mother call her name.

"Need I remind you that my mother was a very dark skinned, very beautiful woman and proud of it. I didn't raise you with a slavery mentality—to buy into society's universal standard of beauty—that whatever looks closest to Caucasian is beautiful. That's what's wrong with blacks now, always trying to measure up to society's standards. Who made them the authority on everything? They even got Asians changing their eyes to appear less ethnic. When will it stop? I'll tell you when it stops, it stops with my daughter. Don't let me hear anything else about how dark you're getting as if that's a bad thing. And you better not ever mention wearing colored contacts to me."

"Okay mom, Jeez, I don't even like colored contacts."

"Well, you better not. Because as I told you before and I'll say it again, changing your eye color is a denial of self. If God had wanted you with green eyes, he would have given them to you!"

"Okay, mom, Jeez! I've got something I need to tell you." Brittany took a moment to gather her thoughts. "Mom, I think I want to talk with students."

Her mother offered a clueless look. "What are you talking about?"

Brittany let out an exaggerated sigh. "Mom, I want to make other students aware of the hidden dangers of Internet dating."

Mrs. Brown turned toward her daughter, her disposition quickly softened. "Oh really, sweetheart?"

Brittany nodded. "I've been thinking about this long and hard and if I can help prevent what happened to me from happening to someone else, then I want to do it."

"Sweetheart, that's really big of you. I'm so proud of you. I'll call Sergeant Jones when we get home."

"No, I'll call him. Mom, you have to start letting me handle my own stuff some. You're not going to be at college with me. Speaking of which, which one am I going to?"

Mrs. Brown stared out into the road and let out a long sigh. "I don't know, Brittany. I don't know what your dad has in mind. With all these changes, I just don't know, sweetheart."

Within weeks, Brittany was scheduled to speak at Stone Mountain High School in DeKalb County. She wasn't ready to face her own school yet. The gymnasium was packed with antsy students. Though Brittany didn't recognize any of the faces seated in the bleachers, she recognized their bored expressions. She patted her face with a facial blotting tissue. Her nerves were in her stomach. She had performed countless times in front of hundred of people at her recitals. But this was different. Speaking to her peers. What if the kids laughed at what she had to say? What if they tuned her out while she was speaking? Officer Liz Petticoat finished her closing remarks and then nodded to Brittany. "The next young lady is going to inform you of the dangers of teen internet dating. Please welcome Brittany Brown to the stage."

A few scattered claps resonated throughout the gym. The kids were unenthused. Brittany stepped to the podium, adjusted her microphone and found a target at the back of the gym—Stone Mountain's high school mascot, a giant eagle painted on the cement wall. The constant hum of chatter continued. "I stand before you today because I am a victim of Internet dating."

All conversations died immediately. The gymnasium

was so quiet, someone could have dropped a penny to the floor and the sound would have reverberated throughout the gym.

"Several weeks ago," Brittany said, "I met a guy on the Internet who was not who he claimed to be." She continued with her story. The kids were mesmerized. To actually see someone who had been a victim was sobering to them. Brittany told the crowd everything that happened. As she brought her speech to a close, she said, "I want to leave you with these final thoughts: One, don't give out personal information. If you feel you've connected with someone online and want to meet in person, get your parents involved. Let them help you decide if it's truly a safe situation. Two, if you do meet someone in person, never go alone. Always have a parent or trusted friend nearby. Three, most of all, remember that people online don't always tell the truth. There are many adults who pose as teenagers to try to get attention, money, or sex. Four, don't give your heart away so quickly. Until you've met them in person, you have no idea what your online friend is really like." Brittany looked out into the crowd. She made eye contact with individual faces. "Please know, this wasn't easy for me to stand before you. But my attacker is still out there, waiting to strike again. And I just don't want it to be you. You all have been a wonderful audience. Thank you."

The crowd clapped and cheered. Brittany thought she even heard a few whistles. She had no idea that speaking to others would be so invigorating and liberating. When she stepped off the podium, boys and girls alike flocked to her, shaking her hand and congratulating her on her courage to speakout and her desire to help others.

Afterwards, Brittany's parents took her to their favorite eatery, Ray's on the River. It had been so long since they had been there. Brittany could already taste the buttery rich bread gliding down her throat. "So, Dad, what are we celebrating?"

"We're celebrating several things tonight: One, what you did this afternoon was very responsible and courageous. It showed a tremendous amount of personal growth. For that, I am proud of you."

Brittany's dimples were so pronounced in her chubby cheeks, they look like two tiny incisions. "Thanks, Daddy. I feel good about it. I just hope they hurry up and catch that creep."

"Sergeant Jones called me today. He said they think that they have him online again. I guess they're doing some undercover sting of some sort. But they won't know for sure. So you still need to be conscious of your surroundings." Her dad smiled. "Now, the second thing we're celebrating. I found an investor."

Brittany mirrored her mom's wide, toothy grin. "So what does that mean for us?" she asked.

"Well, slow your roll. At first I was opposed to an investor, but with one the facility can be completed in roughly nine months—sooner than originally forecasted." Brittany clapped her hands together. "So, does this mean that I can go to Duke?"

"Well, not exactly. We want you to stay in town and go to Emory with your brother."

Brittany's eyes widened. She wondered if she told them that she never turned in her application, if it would ruin their celebration. "No, Daddy, please."

"Well, you've got several good schools right here in town to choose from. Your mom and I have decided that we really don't care which school you choose, but it has to be one here in town."

Tears surfaced in Brittany's eyes. "That's not fair. You guys are trying to keep me from growing up."

"No, we're not."

"Brittany, we just don't want you that far away. If something happens to you or Kevin, we want to know that we can be there at a moment's notice."

"I can't believe you guys. This is so unfair." Brittany's eyes were full of tears. "Why won't you let me grow up?"

Mr. Brown looked around the restaurant. People were beginning to take notice of the conversation that had all of a sudden become heated. "Sheila, go ahead and tell her the good news."

Brittany kept her eyes on the attractive place setting like she didn't even hear them. Nothing mattered anymore. She would never be able to escape the Brown compound. They were probably planning on keeping her there until she was at least thirty and was ready to marry, if they let her marry at all.

"Brittany?" Her mother's voice was sweet.

She refused to look at her.

"Brittany Ann?" her mother said.

Brittany reluctantly looked at her mother, offering a blank distant stare.

"Do you want to hear the good news?"

She smirked. "Whatever."

"Now, the good news is, your father and I have decided to let you stay on the campus of whatever school you decide."

Brittany's doe eyes were wide with surprise. "Really, mom?"

They both nodded. Brittany jumped up from the table, knocking some silverware to the floor and wrapped her arms around her dad. "Thank you, Daddy. So, can I get my car back?"

"Not so fast young lady, we have to see what you are going to do in college. You need to get a job and pay off that credit card."

She let out an exaggerated huff. Her parents were always making her prove herself to them. Well, at least one good thing, she could start counting down the days until she left for college. Brittany grinned as she opened the huge menu and began salivating over the delicious gourmet main dishes.

Chapter 27

When Natasha pulled in front of her mother's house after school, she noticed her dad's car parked in the driveway. It was very odd, because the only person who should have been home was her younger brother, Neil. Her mother usually didn't leave for work until late on most evenings because that's when most of her mom's clients went house shopping. Natasha parked the car and scanned the exterior of the home for visible signs of foul play. No broken windows, kicked in doors, nothing was out of the ordinary except her dad's car. There was only one other thing that it could be, her mom was sick again. Maybe the cancer was out of remission. Four years earlier when the cancer had returned, her father temporarily moved back into the house to help see after the family. It was good, but in some ways, it gave the children a false sense of hope. Natasha and Neil assumed their parents would be getting back together and when it didn't happen, Neil was very angry. Now, Natasha braced herself as she approached the garage door that led into the kitchen. Her parents were seated at the kitchen table, sipping coffee.

That, too, was strange. Her mom hated coffee. "Hey, sweet pea," her mom said, her voice full and vibrant as usual. She met her mother's gaze. Much to her surprise, her mother was smiling.

"Hi Mom, hey Dad."

"Hey princess, how was school?"

"Fine." Natasha had no desire to continue with the small talk. She wanted to get it over with.

"Sweet pea, have a seat. Your dad and I have something we'd like to talk to you about."

Natasha glanced at her father and then back to her mother. She slowly sat down in the seat next to him since it appeared her mother was going to be doing all the talking.

"Breath, girl!" her mom said with a smile.

"What!" Natasha snapped. "I don't know what's going on here."

"Your dad and I have decided . . ."

Her mother paused. Natasha glared at her, annoyed with her jovial antics.

"Lighten up, sweetie," her mother said. Natasha still refused to smile. "We have decided to let you go to Paris!"

"What!" Natasha's heart flooded with joy. "Are you serious?"

"Yes, we're serious," her dad responded.

Natasha shot around to the other side of the table and wrapped her long, slender arms around her mom's neck, nearly choking her with love. Then, she hugged her dad with the same forcefulness. "Ohmigod! What made you change your minds?"

"Well, Tasha, I thought about it long and hard. You

have always been an outstanding student. I don't believe you've ever come home with a C, have you?"

"No, ma'am," Natasha quickly added to help plead her case.

"You've always been very responsible. I think you'll take care of yourself. You speak the language. Monsieur Marais called and reassured us that he would keep a very close watch on you. He said that he would call me once a week to let me know how things are going."

"Wow! So what about college?"

"Princess," her father said lovingly, "We've decided to give you an opportunity to do something different. Explore the world. You've always been a very level-headed person, so I know that if you see things are not working out with modeling as you hoped, you'll come home and go to college."

"Yes, daddy, I plan on still going to college anyway. I know I can't model forever." Tears began to stream down Natasha's cheeks. She had no idea her parents had that much confidence and faith in her. "Thank you so much," she said with genuine gratitude.

Her mother smiled. "You're welcome. You deserve all the wonderful things that life has to offer. And you're going to have an extremely high phone bill. And I mean you, not me. That's going to be your expense. You'll be required to call me every day until I start to feel more comfortable."

"Okay, mom," Natasha offered reassuringly. "May I please go call my friends to tell them the news?"

"Yes, but give your father a hug goodbye. He's leaving."

Natasha hugged her dad and jetted upstairs to her bedroom. She was so happy, she didn't know who she should call first, Shaniqua or Brittany. She thought of calling Stephen, but she wanted to tell him the good news in person. She dialed Shaniqua's number and then dialed Brittany's to get them on a three-way call.

Chapter 28

So many days had passed since Shaniqua had last been to work that it actually felt good to get ready to go to the store. She hadn't felt like dressing and fixing herself up since her grandmother's funeral. It was a relief to think about something other than her little life. She was nervous when she first arrived. She knew Ursula was waiting to tear into her. The store was brightly lit and packed with kids as usual. Shaniqua waved to Cindy, who was behind the cash register, and went straight to the back. Ursula, a stocky figure in all black, had her hands resting over the rolls in her waistline. "Oh, so you finally decided to show up, huh? If it had been up to me, I would have fired yo' little tired behind a long time ago."

With her nostrils flared with anger, Shaniqua stared at her hard, trying to understand how this grown woman had the audacity to antagonize her. Shaniqua rolled her eyes and then slammed her locker shut. Ursula was so not worth the effort. She was a cruel, heartless pig, Shaniqua thought, as she made her way to the register where Cindy was waiting with a big welcoming smile and open arms. "Hey, hon, how are you?"

Her lips parted into a soft smile. "Good."

"I'm really sorry about your grandmother. If there's anything I can do, just let me know."

"Thanks, Cindy."

"Now that you are back, I have some other business to attend. I'll be in the back for a little while. Can you handle things out here by yourself?"

"Sure," Shaniqua replied. But she really wanted to say, "Send Ursula's fat turkey legs out here."

Twenty minutes later, Ursula emerged from the back room. With nostrils flared like a bull's, she stormed through the store and out into the mall. Cindy joined Shaniqua behind the cash register. Shaniqua looked puzzled. "What in the world is her problem?"

"Let's just say, she won't be back here."

A smile crept across Shaniqua's face. "Really!" she caught the excitement in her own voice. "I mean sorry to hear that."

"For the last two months, I've been having trouble balancing the sales sheets," Cindy said. "We have not charged her with anything, but she can no longer work here."

Too bad, so sad, Shaniqua thought. "Well, I'm going to

miss her."

"You lie!" Cindy said, laughing.

"You're right, I'm lying," she said and started praise dancing. "Hallelujah!"

After work, Shaniqua stretched out on the couch when all of a sudden she heard two voices giggling like school kids. One voice she could easily make out, it was her cousin's Nee Nee's. But the other voice was unfamiliar. Shaniqua raised up and pulled the blanket over her bare legs. She had been relaxing in boxer shorts and a tank top all evening. The apartment door sprang open. Nee Nee was visibly drunk and so was an old, balding man who looked like he had been drinking pints of liquor for breakfast, lunch and dinner for all fifty plus years of his life.

"What's up, girl?" Nee Nee said. "That's my baby cousin." She dropped her purse to the floor and quickly grabbed three beers from the refrigerator, handing one to her cousin. Shaniqua thought about taking it. It's not like there was anyone there to tell her not to. But she gently pushed it back toward her cousin.

"Girl, here, take this damn beer."

Something inside of Shaniqua wouldn't let her. She jumped off the couch, grabbed her sneakers and purse and left the apartment. That lonely feeling was gnawing at her. Granny's voice ricocheted between her ears, "You know that chile's up to no good. You stick around her long enough, you'll be just like her. Mark my words, chile. Just like her."

Her brisk walk slowed to a snail's pace and then not at all. Taking a seat at the nearby bus stop, Shaniqua began frantically searching her purse. Moments later, the Navy brochure emerged. Using the light from the street lamp above, she studied the brochure with extreme intensity, reading it in its entirety. The benefits were remarkable. Travel. Education. Independence. Suddenly, Shaniqua whipped out her cell phone and dialed nurse Cassandra's number. "Hello, Ms. Cassandra. This is Shaniqua, Bessie Williams' granddaughter. You said to call you if I needed some information. Can you help me get into the Navy?"

Cassandra's voice was soft and reassuring. "Sugar, I think that's an excellent choice. You still interested in nursing?"

"Yes, ma'am. I think I would like to try it."

"I think you would be excellent. You have so much to gain and you can start building your nursing career now. You can be an officer. Your opinions will matter to fellow nurses, doctors, surgeons. It's a great profession. But most importantly, you possess the ability to touch people's lives on a daily basis."

Shaniqua listened intently as Cassandra helped her construct a plan. When they finished, she closed the phone and looked into the night sky. A warm, peaceful feeling clothed her from the chilly air. Life was worth living. She had to live well because her grandmother was watching from above.

Chapter 29

The following day at school, Shaniqua entered with an energetic stride. She now had a plan, a vision for her life. Her friends were waiting in the commons area. She looked at Brittany and Natasha, her eyes dancing between them. "What's up, ladies? How y'all doing this beautiful, sunshiny morning?"

Brittany leaned in closer and tugged Shaniqua's skin on her forearm.

"Ouch! What are you doing?"

"I'm trying to see who this imposter is, because you always have something smart to say," Brittany scoffed.

"Girl, please. You always got your mouth turned up like you sucking on sour lemons. Tell her, Tasha."

Natasha's eyes darted between them. "Ohmigod, you guys have got to be kidding me. Stop, please."

Shaniqua draped her arm around Brittany's shoulder. "Girl, you know I love this ol' sourpuss!" she said, "Give me y'alls yearbooks, I didn't get a chance to sign them."

"Oops! Tasha, I need your keys, I left mine in your car this morning."

Shaniqua looked at Brittany inquisitively. "Why'd you do that?"

"My, aren't we being awfully nosey? Tasha gave me a ride to school. Is that okay with you?"

"Where's your car, Brit?"

Brittany turned to Natasha for the answer. Natasha responded with an encouraging smile. "It's okay, go ahead and tell her."

Brittany drew in a deep breath. "I don't have a car anymore," she said, staring at the terrazzo flooring, waiting for Shaniqua to cackle like a hyena as usual.

Shaniqua wrapped her arm around Brittany. "It's okay, girl. We've known for awhile now."

Brittany smirked to hide her embarrassment. "Why didn't you say something?"

Shaniqua shrugged. "What's there to say? Shoot, everybody has financial problems."

"We don't have financial problems," Brittany snapped. "My dad's trying to build a new medical facility."

"Okay, Brit, whatever. The point is, we loved your raggedy tail when you didn't have a car and we still love your raggedy, well . . . most days."

The bell rang and all three friends headed to class.

Shaniqua sat down in English 4 with Natasha's yearbook out

in the open. Since it was the last day of school, teachers didn't care. Everyone was swapping yearbooks around the room. As Shaniqua collected her thoughts, she suddenly became overwhelmed with emotion. She hoped a tear wouldn't surface.

Natasha Elaine Harris,

What can I say? We finally made it to our senior year. We've been together since the third grade. We've watched each other change and grow. You used to be a tomboy, yes, I said it, yes I did! But look at you now, you are a beautiful young lady. Got the brothas fighting over you! Anyway, we've been through good times and the bad ones. Just think, we laughed together and cried together. I can't imagine anyone having as much fun together as we did. You have gotten me through some pretty difficult times and you have also given me inspiration. What more can a friend give than that? Keep your head up high and I bet that you'll be a big success in the future.

Love Always,

Shaniqua Williams

When she finished writing, she discreetly caught the tear that slowly crept down her face. Natasha had always been there for her, never judging her the way others did. Shaniqua smiled through tear-stained eyes. She had received pure, unconditional love from two people in the world, Granny and Natasha.

Chapter 30

Sheathed in a pale yellow, strapless dress, Brittany was strikingly beautiful. Her mom had surprised her with a designer dress from her favorite New York boutique for graduation. Brittany glowed in the passenger seat beside her mom on the way to the ceremony. Her brother Kevin and her dad were meeting them at the school. Brittany was smiling so hard and unsophisticatedly, her cheeks burned with happiness. "Mom, you know what, I'm really looking forward to college."

"Good. Do you have any idea what you want to study?"

Brittany thought about telling her mom what she assumed she wanted to hear—medicine. Instead, she decided on the truth. "No, not yet."

"Well, that's okay, honey. You have plenty of time."

She shot her mother a curious glance. She wasn't expecting such a nonchalant response. "Really?"

"Really. At age eighteen, very few people really know what they want to do professionally. So, my advice to you in college, is to take as many different courses as you can to see what really interests you. For instance, when I was in college, I studied pre-law, but I took a Women's Literature class as an elective. I really loved that class. It's the only class that I worked ahead and was curious about readings that weren't even assigned." Mrs. Brown's voice was soft. "In hindsight, I wished I had pursued a degree in Literature."

"Mom, it's never too late. Isn't that what you and Daddy always tell us?"

"Well, that's different," Mrs. Brown retorted.

"No, mom, it isn't. You can do and become anything you want at any age. You can't give up on your dreams."

Mrs. Brown pulled into the crowded school parking lot. "Gosh, you know you're getting old when your kids start lecturing you."

They both giggled and went inside the building.

Natasha donned a sleek, turquoise, off-the-shoulder dress with matching stilettos. She felt herself growing more enthralled with fashion. The latest Vogue magazine was always clutched in her hands. Monsieur Marais told her that it was essential to know who was who in the modeling industry. She knew which model had which contracts, which designers favored which models. She ingeniously studied poses, photographers and learned which products booked which model types.

After sliding on a series of gold bangles around her wrist, she took a long look in the mirror, looking deep into her eyes as she had never seen herself before. She looked past the prettiness that was staring back at her and moved closer to the mirror, studying the intensity burning through her eyes, venturing into the soul of herself. She had no idea where her aspirations would lead her, but she knew with certainty, graduation night was the beginning of the rest of her adult life and she was going to live it without regret. Natasha smiled and closed her bedroom door behind her.

Shaniqua had dozed off to sleep on the couch waiting for her Aunt Kathy and Nee Nee to pick her up for graduation. Shaniqua tossed and turned on the black leather sofa, her vision was clouded, but she felt something tugging at her wrist. It felt like her grandmother's strong hand. Suddenly, she was frozen still by the sound of her grandmother's voice. "Baby, it's Granny. Sorry I couldn't be there to see you graduate. Nothing makes me more proud. You gonna make something of yo'self. I knows 'cause I been prayin' for a long time. This is all according to God's plan." A tear streaked down Shaniqua's cheek. She wrapped her hand around her grandmother's tightly as if she never wanted to let her go. A car horn honked, waking her from her dream. "Tell that chile I'm gonna skin her hide!"

Shaniqua smiled and closed Nee Nee's apartment door behind her. She couldn't believe that at her most proud moment ever, Granny wasn't able to share in it. Out of all of Granny's children and grandchildren, she was the one who finally finished high school. She didn't expect her mother to be present. She was probably in Baltimore, in someone's hellhole.

When they arrived at school, the gymnasium was filled to capacity. Students and parents were posing for pictures. The gym clamored with the noisy excitement of three hundred graduating seniors. One by one, the students took the stage to receive their graduation diploma. They all took turns cheering for one another. When it was Shaniqua's turn, she took her diploma, shook Principal Canada's hand and blew a big kiss in the air to her grandmother.

At the end of the ceremony, Brittany, Natasha and Shaniqua gathered for pictures. Shaniqua stood in between her two best friends and hugged them. Tears of joy and sadness were cascading down all the girls' faces.

"Y'all," Natasha said, "we're going to be different from everyone else. We're going to hold on to our friendship. Pinky promise?" Natasha struck her fingers in the air.

Brittany curled her stubby finger around Natasha's. "I'm going to be right down at Spelman, so y'all can't lose touch with me."

"Friends to the end, no matter how far the Navy sends me across the oceans," Shaniqua added. "I promise to always stay in touch."

"And no matter how big of a super model I become," Natasha said.

Brittany and Shaniqua stuck their index fingers in front of Natasha's face, and said in unison "Riiiiiiight!" while Mrs. Brown snapped a picture.

After the girls said their goodbyes to one another, Brittany and her brother Kevin trailed their parents out to the parking lot. They were in a deep conversation about how to keep their parents off their backs at college, when Brittany called out, "Mom, I'm going to ride with Kevin over to the restaurant."

"No, you're not!" she yelled.

Brittany shot her brother an "I-told-you-so" look. Kevin smiled, which angered her even more. She wondered if he liked that they treated her differently than him. She looked around for her best friends—she'd rather be with them than her own family, she thought. "Mom, why can't I ride with him?"

"Because," her mom said, steadily walking, "wouldn't you like to drive your own car?"

Brittany puckered her brows in confusion, scanning the parking lot. Her eyes fell on a big white bow on the hood of a gold Lexus ES 350 a couple of yards away. "What! Are you kidding me?" she said, sprinting to the car. "Is this mine?"

"Yep!" her dad said, "All you have to cover is the insurance."

"For real?"

Both of her parents chuckled. "Congratulations!" her dad said.

She quickly hugged them and excitedly inspected her new ride.

Shaniqua decided to go out to dinner with Natasha's family since Nee Nee had to go to work. They enjoyed a fabulous dinner at the Cheesecake Factory. After dinner, Natasha decided to spend some time with Stephen and let her brother, Nate, take Shaniqua home.

Natasha rode alongside Stephen. The hot air had a relaxing effect on her skin. She was waiting for the right time to tell him about her future plans. Things had been going very well between them lately. Maybe he sensed he had been smothering her and decided to let up a bit. Stephen held Natasha's hand in his while he steered the car with the other one. "So what do you want to do tonight? A bunch of kids are having a party tonight. I'm game if you are," he said.

"That's cool, but Stephen, can we talk first?"

"Shoot."

"Well, can you pull over for a minute?"

He parked on a dark residential street in Buckhead.

"Well, Stephen, I was waiting to tell you the good news tonight."

"What good news?"

"My parents are letting me go to Paris in August?"

"Wow! You're going back so soon."

"This time I'm going back to work as a model."

"For real, Tasha!"

She witnessed Stephen's smile, but somehow it didn't seem sincere. "What's the matter?"

"Nothing, I'm happy for you. I'm sure you'll do very well." Stephen tried to hide his disappointment out of the window. He stared into the darkness for a long time.

"What's the matter? I thought you out of all people would be thrilled for me. I owe this all to you. I never in a million years would have thought of modeling if you hadn't painted that portrait of me over two years ago."

Stephen's breathing was uneven. He definitely was trying to arrange his thoughts into words. After a long awkward silence, he spoke. "So what's going to happen to us?"

"What do you mean?"

"I mean, how's this going to work for us? You being over in another country. I thought we were going to go to the University of Georgia together."

"Stephen, I never told you that I was going to UGA. Why would I want to go there when my brother Nate goes there? College is a time when you're suppose to try to become your own person. I want to get away from the whole Nate-Natasha b-ball thing."

Stephen clenched his jaw.

"Everything's going to work out just fine." Natasha clasped her hands in her lap nonchalantly. "Watch."

"I'm not feeling this."

Her face twisted. "What?"

"This. Us. You."

She couldn't believe what she was actually hearing. Was he serious? He couldn't be. Why was he making a big deal of them not going off to school together?

Stephen cranked the engine and without hesitation, whipped the car back onto the road. He made a quick U-turn.

"Where are we going?"

"I'm taking you home."

"Just like that?"

"This is not going to work. Our lives are headed in two different directions. And you obviously don't have room for someone like me in yours."

"Stephen, what are you talking about? I haven't changed. I'm the same Tasha from two, three years ago."

"Well, it's just a matter of time before you leave me for someone else."

At first, Natasha was sad, but now anger was slowly overtaking her. Was this why he started acting jealous and possessive, because of his own insecurities? She really didn't know what to say. Maybe they needed to break up, she thought. That way she would be free to date whoever, whenever. She was too young to be saddled with another person's issues. "Well, I'm sorry you feel that way."

"Yep, I am too."

They continued the rest of the ride in silence. When Stephen pulled up in front of Natasha's house, she grabbed her purse from the floor and opened the car door.

"Wait," he said. His voice quivered.

She glowered at him. His eyes were full of tears,

causing hers to tear up, too. She had loved Stephen in the two years that they had been a couple. She had even toyed with the idea of losing her virginity to him, after she turned eighteen and was away in college. He was her first love. Without warning, Natasha felt something tugging at her heart. She wrapped her arms around Stephen. The tears poured. She kissed him on the mouth. Both of their tears were on each other's face. "Stephen, I'll always love you."

He nodded. He was too choked up to speak. After awhile, Stephen spoke slowly and deliberately. "I'll always love you too, Tasha. If ever you need me, just call or shoot me an e-mail." He looked deep into her eyes. "Tasha, I really am happy for you."

"Thanks, Stephen."

They embraced one another to help ease the pain and said their goodbyes.

Natasha entered the house, she had no idea breaking up was going to be so hard. She wondered if they were making a wrong decision. Her mom greeted her at the door. "Oh, sweet pea, what's wrong?"

"Stephen and I just broke up."

"Oh, baby, I'm sorry. What happened?"

"Nothing. We just decided that our lives are going

into two different directions and I'm not ready to be so serious and get engaged and whatever else."

"Well, baby, if it's meant to be, it'll be."

"I know, mom, but it really hurts."

"Breaking up always does. There's no easy way around it. You just have to go through it. I remember when I was your age, I dated a guy and we broke up and I swore to my mother that I would never love like that again. But you know what, sweetheart, Father Time heals all wounds." Her mother grabbed a tissue from the kitchen counter and wiped her daughter's mascara-stained cheeks.

Natasha smiled through the tears, the heartache. "Thanks, Mom," she said, and pulled away from her mother and made her way to her bedroom. She desperately wanted to be alone to think and cry, and cry and think, without distractions. Stephen was the sweetest guy she had ever known.

Shaniqua sat quietly in the car as Nate drove. She didn't know what to say to him. They had never been alone before. Natasha had always been the common link. Maybe it was best not to speak at all. She hid her nervousness out the car window while she thought about how college had definitely done him justice. He had grown taller and more buffed. People complained about freshmen putting on weight, but the added poundage looked good on him, she thought.

"So, Shaniqua, you want to hang out a little? I mean it's your graduation night. Nobody goes home on graduation night," Nate said, smiling over at her.

His voice startled her, snapping her out of her trance. Her nerves wouldn't allow her to even look at him. "I guess so," she said, hiding her smile out the car window.

"So, what do you want to do?"

Shaniqua shrugged as if she had temporarily lost her voice. She finally allowed her eyes to meet his. He looked so handsome dressed in a black suit, black shirt, black tie—Mafia style. Gangsta, Shaniqua thought.

"Am I keeping you from someone?" She shook her head. "Good, then let's go to the fair."

"The fair?" Shaniqua said, looking down at her fitted, pink halter dress. "Like this?"

"We'll get changed."

"The fair?"

"It'll be fun!" Nate said, smiling. "I promise."

Nate patiently waited in the car for Shaniqua to change out of her dress and into jean shorts, a red eye candy top and flip-flops. Then they drove to Nate's house, all the while chatting easily about college life and her plans for the future. He was so nice and easy going that she found herself talking about her grandmother and, for the first time, without crying. He listened as though he really cared. She couldn't help but wonder why he was being so nice to her. Maybe he felt sorry that she didn't have anyone to be with on graduation night like everyone else.

When they pulled into the driveway, Shaniqua saw Natasha's bedroom light on. "I thought Tasha was hanging out with Stephen tonight."

"Come on in," Nate said. "You can visit her, while I get changed."

She trailed him into the house and up the stairs. She was outside her best friend's bedroom door when she heard the radio, but she also thought she heard sniffling. Shaniqua tapped on the door. "Go away, Neil, I'm busy!"

"Tasha, it's me," Shaniqua whispered. "Can I come in?"

Natasha quickly tried to clean her face using the inside of the comforter. "Yeah, girl. What are you doing here?"

When Shaniqua opened the door, she saw the puffiness in her friend's eyes. She rushed to the bed. "What's wrong?"

Natasha shook her head. "Stephen and I are over."

"Oh, I'm sorry, Tasha. Girl, what did he do?"

"He didn't do anything. We just decided that our lives are not headed in the same direction."

"Oh, I'm sorry. Are you going to be all right?"

Natasha nodded. "What are you doing here anyway?"

"Nate and I are going to the fair."

Natasha looked at Shaniqua curiously.

"Don't trip. It's not even like that. We're just friends hanging out," Shaniqua said, smiling. "Don't worry about

Stephen. It'll be alright. In the words of my grandmother, 'Sometimes, you have to love something enough to be willing to let it go.'"

They held each other for a long time. No words could express what their friendship had meant to one another over the years.

Minutes later, Nate had changed his clothes and they were driving to the Fulton County fairgrounds where he whipped out his wallet and bought enough tickets for the both of them. "So, what do you want to ride first?"

Shaniqua looked at the giant swing, then the hang glider, and then the Scorpion. "I'm not getting on these raggedy rides. Boy, you crazy?"

Nate chuckled. "What you scurred?"

"No, I'm not scurred."

He draped his arm around her shoulders. She immediately felt the sparks travel to her heart. She wondered if he was taking a personal interest in her or if he was just being a gentleman. She immediately shook the thought away. He was away in college with college girls. Not to mention he knew her business from a couple of years ago. He knew all about Jordan and what went down between them. He had been the one to come to her rescue when Jordan was trying to fight her. A smile came to her mouth when she recalled how Nate clocked Jordan in the jaw and knocked him to the floor in front of everybody.

Nate slowly guided her over to the Ferris wheel. "Look, let's just try this and if you don't like it, we don't have to ride anymore." He extended his hand to Shaniqua. "Deal?"

She grinned. "Deal."

Moments later, she climbed into the car of the Ferris wheel. Nate sat down beside her and began rocking. "Boy, have you lost your mind. Don't even play like that!"

When the ride slowly moved to allow for the other riders to board, Shaniqua gripped the bar forcefully with both hands. He chuckled, and then she chuckled along to play it off.

Nate took a long look at Shaniqua. "So, how come you're not out with your boyfriend?"

Shaniqua made a face. "Boyfriend? I don't have a boyfriend."

"Okay, don't bite my head off. I'm just making conversation."

Embarrassment washed over her. Maybe she was being overly sensitive on the subject. But she was still trying so hard to shake the bad image that everyone had of her. Maybe Nate was different. He always seemed to be. "So, where's your girlfriend?" Shaniqua asked nervously.

"I was dating someone at school," Nate replied casually. "But we broke up,"

Curiosity was upon her. She wanted to know why, but Granny's words echoed in her head, "Curiosity killed the cat." And Shaniqua would always respond, "But satisfaction brought it back!" She had to know why they broke up. Nate wasn't a dog. Not even close to it. She had only remembered him dating one girl, a nobody named Ariel. Actually, now that she thought about it, they dated for a couple of years, even though Ariel had left the school after her junior year to attend a private school. Shaniqua toyed with her fingers trying to decide if she should be nosey. Forget curiosity killing the cat—it was killing her. "Why'd y'all break up?"

He offered a nonchalant shrug. "We just didn't make it."

"Well, what happened?"

"Hmmm, let's see. Well, her boyfriend came to the school to help her move out of the dorm and drove her back home to Milwaukee, Wisconsin."

Shaniqua wasn't sure what to say. "Ohhh."

The Ferris wheel started moving. A loud high-pitched squeal escaped Shaniqua, prompting her to grab onto Nate. The smell of sweet musk tickled her nose. Then she squealed again, this time moving closer to him. He wrapped his arm around her securely as they went around, and around and around. It felt so good to be in his arms. Secure. With the night air hovering all around her, she felt so alive, so free, so secure. She could ride the Ferris wheel forever.

When Nate pulled up in front of Shaniqua's house, she thought quietly to herself that this was the absolute best date she had ever had. Even if it wasn't a real date, she was going to remember it that way. Remember what it felt like to have a guy treat her with respect. She could feel him staring at her. "Good luck, with the Navy and nursing school," Nate said. "I think you're going to make a great nurse."

Shaniqua smiled, but disappointment had framed her face. She had definitely read more into the situation. "Thanks, Nate, thanks for everything, and good luck with basketball at UGA," she said, getting out of the car.

"Ouch!" Nate yelled.

She leaned back down and looked into the car. "Are you alright?"

"No, as a matter of fact, I got a cut on my ankle. Can I bring it by tomorrow to let you take a look?"

Shaniqua blushed.

You Are Worthy of Greatness

These things I say you should take to heart
and consider the possibilities of a brand new start.
Don't ever let anyone set goals for your life
or you'll always end up with struggles and strife.

These words I say to you are true
so when you're feeling down and feeling blue,
keep your head up, heart open and think things
through.
Don't ever let anyone determine your worth
or put you down and make you feel like dirt.

Keep your eyes on the prize and your head to the sky
and I promise these words will always get you by.

— Carmen Cooper

Eye Candy
Discussion Guide

- What was the most interesting event in the book and why?

- Who was your favorite or least favorite character(s) and why?

- What are your thoughts about Brittany meeting Dante through the Internet? If it were you, how would you prevent what happened?

- Describe the life changing events Shaniqua experienced.

- How do you feel about Shaniqua's decision to join the military?

- What type of relationship did Natasha and Stephen have?

- How did the relationship between Natasha and Stephen change?

- What are the positive and/or negative aspects of Natasha pursuing a modeling career instead of attending college?

- Identify the role model in each girl's life. How did his/her actions influenced the character's life?

- What are the benefits of having short and long-term goals?

T-Shirt Giveaway

One lucky reader will be selected every month to receive a free T-shirt.

❏ *Ms. Thang* fitted T-shirt
Size: ❏ S   ❏ M   ❏ L   ❏ XL

❏ *Urban Goddess* fitted T-shirt
Size: ❏ S   ❏ M   ❏ L   ❏ XL

❏ *Eye Candy* fitted T-shirt
Size: ❏ S   ❏ M   ❏ L   ❏ XL

Please submit this page to enter. Duplicate entries or photocopies will not be accepted. Please print legibly. You will be notified via e-mail.

Name:_____

Address:_____

City _____State_____Zip_____-___

Email:_____

Please Mail to:
NUA Multimedia
2657-G Annapolis Road, Suite 233
Hanover, MD 21076

GOOD LUCK!

Other books by Sonia Hayes:

Book I
Ms. Thang
ISBN 978-0-9777573-0-5

Book II
Urban Goddess
ISBN 978-0-9777573-1-2

Book III
Eye Candy
ISBN 978-0-9777573-2-9

Q U I C K   O R D E R   F O R M

Fax order: 410.487.6461. *(Send this form.)*
E-mail order: orders@nuamultimedia.com
Postal order: NUA Multimedia
                          2657-G Annapolis Road
                          Suite 233
                          Hanover, MD 21076. USA

Have your credit card ready.

Please send the following:

❑ *Ms. Thang* Novel ($9.95 ea.)
❑ *Urban Goddess* Novel ($9.95 ea.)
❑ *Eye Candy* Novel ($9.95 ea.)
❑ *Ms. Thang* fitted T-shirt – Size S, M, L, XL ($14.95 ea.)
❑ *Urban Goddess* fitted T-shirt – Size S, M, L, XL ($14.95 ea.)
❑ *Eye Candy* fitted T-shirt – Size S, M, L, XL ($14.95 ea.)

Special Offer – Buy one book and one shirt for $20.00

Please mail to:

Name:_____

Address:_____

City _____State____Zip_____-_____

Telephone: _____

Email: _____

Shipping by air:

❑ US: $4 for the first product and $2 for each additional product.
❑ International: $9 for the first product and $5 for each additional
    product. (estimate)

Payment: ❑ Money Order   ❑ Check   ❑ Credit card:
                 ❑ Visa ❑ MasterCard ❑ AMEX ❑ Discover

Card number _____

Name on card _____Exp. Date_____

Signature _____